# Titles by *Langaa* RPCIG

**Francis B. Nyamnjoh**
Stories from Abakwa
Mind Searching
The Disillusioned African
The Convert
Souls Forgotten
Married But Available

**Dibussi Tande**
No Turning Back. Poems of Freedom 1990-1993
Scribbles from the Den: Essays on Politics and Collecti
Memory in Cameroon

**Kangsen Feka Wakai**
Fragmented Melodies

**Ntemfac Ofege**
Namondo. Child of the Water Spirits
Hot Water for the Famous Seven

**Emmanuel Fru Doh**
Not Yet Damascus
The Fire Within
Africa's Political Wastelands: The Bastardization of
Cameroon
Oriki'badan
Wading the Tide

**Thomas Jing**
Tale of an African Woman

**Peter Wuteh Vakunta**
Grassfields Stories from Cameroon
Green Rape: Poetry for the Environment
Majunga Tok: Poems in Pidgin English
Cry, My Beloved Africa
No Love Lost
Straddling The Mungo: A Book of Poems in English &
French

**Ba'bila Mutia**
Coils of Mortal Flesh

**Kehbuma Langmia**
Titabet and the Takumbeng
An Evil Meal of Evil

**Victor Elame Musinga**
The Barn
The Tragedy of Mr. No Balance

**Ngessimo Mathe Mutaka**
Building Capacity: Using TEFL and African Languages as
Development-oriented Literacy Tools

**Milton Krieger**
Cameroon's Social Democratic Front: Its History and
Prospects as an Opposition Political Party, 1990-2011

**Sammy Oke Akombi**
The Raped Amulet
The Woman Who Ate Python
Beware the Drives: Book of Verse

**Susan Nkwentie Nde**
Precipice
Second Engagement

**Francis B. Nyamnjoh &
Richard Fonteh Akum**
The Cameroon GCE Crisis: A Test of Anglophone
Solidarity

**Joyce Ashuntantang & Dibussi Tande**
Their Champagne Party Will End! Poems in Honor of
Bate Besong

**Emmanuel Achu**
Disturbing the Peace

T0209649

**Albert Azeyeh**
Réussite scolaire, faillite sociale : généalogie mentale de
la crise de l'Afrique noire francophone

**Aloysius Ajab Amin & Jean-Luc Dubois**
Croissance et développement au Cameroun :
d'une croissance équilibrée à un développement équitable

**Carlson Anyangwe**
Imperialistic Politics in Cameroun:
Resistance & the Inception of the Restoration of the
Statehood of Southern Cameroons

**Bill F. Ndi**
K'Cracy, Trees in the Storm and Other Poems
Map: Musings On Ars Poetica
Thomas Lurting: The Fighting Sailor Turn'd Peaceable /
Le marin combattant devenu paisible

**Kathryn Toure, Therese Mungah
Shalo Tchombe & Thierry Karsenti**
ICT and Changing Mindsets in Education

**Charles Alobwed'Epie**
The Day God Blinked

**G.D. Nyamndi**
Babi Yar Symphony
Whether losing, Whether winning
Tussles: Collected Plays

**Samuel Ebelle Kingue**
Si Dieu était tout un chacun de nous?

**Ignasio Malizani Jimu**
Urban Appropriation and Transformation : bicycle, taxi
and handcart operators in Mzuzu, Malawi

**Justice Nyo' Wakai:**
Under the Broken Scale of Justice: The Law and My
Times

**John Eyong Mengot**
A Pact of Ages

**Ignasio Malizani Jimu**
Urban Appropriation and Transformation: Bicycle Taxi
and Handcart Operators

**Joyce B. Ashuntantang**
Landscaping and Coloniality: The Dissemination of
Cameroon Anglophone Literature

**Jude Fokwang**
Mediating Legitimacy: Chieftaincy and Democratisation in
Two African Chiefdoms

**Michael A. Yanou**
Dispossession and Access to Land in South Africa: an
African Perspevctive

**Tikum Mbah Azonga**
Cup Man and Other Stories

**John Nkemngong Nkengasong**
Letters to Marions (And the Coming Generations)

**Amady Aly Dieng**
Les étudiants africains et la littérature négro-africaine
d'expression française

**Tah Asongwed**
Born to Rule: Autobiography of a life President

**Frida Menkan Mbunda**
Shadows From The Abyss

**Bongasu Tanla Kishani**
A Basket of Kola Nuts

**Fo Angwafo III S.A.N of Mankon**
Royalty and Politics: The Story of My Life

**Basil Diki**
The Lord of Anomy

**Churchill Ewumbue-Monono**
Youth and Nation-Building in Cameroon: A Study of
National Youth Day Messages and Leadership Discourse
(1949-2009)

**Emmanuel N. Chia, Joseph C. Suh & Alexandre
Ndeffo Tene**
Perspectives on Translation and Interpretation in
Cameroon

**Linus T. Asong**
The Crown of Thorns

**Vivian Sihshu Yenika**
Imitation Whiteman

**Beatrice Fri Bime**
Someplace, Somewhere

# Someplace, Somewhere

### Beatrice Fri Bime

Langaa Research & Publishing CIG
Mankon, Bamenda

Publisher:
*Langaa* RPCIG
Langaa Research & Publishing Common Initiative Group
P.O. Box 902 Mankon
Bamenda
North West Region
Cameroon
Langaagrp@gmail.com
www.langaa-rpcig.net


Distributed outside N. America by African Books Collective
orders@africanbookscollective.com
www.africanbookscollective.com


Distributed in N. America by Michigan State University
Press
msupress@msu.edu
www.msupress.msu.edu


ISBN: 9956-558-92-3

## DISCLAIMER

*The names, characters, places and incidents in this book are either the product of the author's imagination or are used fictitiously. Accordingly, any resemblance to actual persons, living or dead, events, or locales is entirely one of incredible coincidence.*

# Contents

# Dedication

To **KININLA,** whose name set the tone and pace of her life. Kininla, may you rest in perfect peace.

To the people who have made me the person that I am:

- My grandmother, **Sarah Angob Mbaku**, who truly instilled in me the principles of life;

- My mother, **Elizabeth Anje Mbaku**, who gave birth to me and nurtured me;

- My Uncle, **John Chiawah Mbaku,** who sacrificed a lot for me;

- My husband, **John Sabbas Bime**, who taught me the meaning of love.

You live on in my heart.

To Kerman, Chiawa and Akere Bime, for the pleasure of being your mother. I love you.

# Acknowledgements

This book would not have been possible without contributions in one form or the other from the following:

Grace Kuaban, Caroline Kilo Bara, Evelyn Kininla Nkerbu, Caro Nsai, Susan Bamu Apara, Florence Ndinyah, Julius Sama Ndi, Lorraine Mbaku, Yvonne, Florence, Sandrine, Anye Mbaku, Marriana Maimo and Asheri Kilo.

Thanks to Mary Sevidzem, Stella and Roland Mbenkum, Gwen and Geoffrey Mbaku, Christy and Nelson Fomenky, for their constant support.

Heartfelt appreciation to my editors, Dr. Viban Ngo, Mathias Ofon, Aisatou Ngong, and Jude Waindim. Thank you for making the work better.

Special thanks to Mr. Brian McCabe, my mentor on The British Council "Crossing Borders" programme, for your encouragement and feedback; and most especially to The British Council Cameroon, the Cameroon Ministry of Culture, and CYBERLINE, for taking this work to the public.

# Someplace, Somewhere

# Chapter One

The family sat in the living room watching television. Two rats, Flunky and Redd, came out of their holes and sat under the chairs and watched television too. Redd and Flunky sat on their hind legs, talking quietly when their attention was drawn to the evening news. The major news item was that Aloh Urban Council had bought a fleet of trucks and garbage vans from the Renault Motor Company in their bid to keep the city clean.

The rats laughed, "shi-shi shi-shi," and of course, their presence was made known to the family. The family continued watching the screen, indifferent to the presence of the rats, but one person got up, grasped a broom and waged an ever-losing battle against the rats.

Flunky and Redd were very good friends, but they were from different families of rats. Flunky was a small field rat with thin dark fur who ran in the field and frequented the accumulated garbage in the streets. Redd, the house rat, was clean and fat, with fair fur.

Redd always felt superior to Flunky and sometimes looked down on him because of his scavenging and vagabond nature. However, Redd and Flunky had been friends for a very long time and respected each other because both of them were clan chiefs. After Flunky's two-week absence, they were meeting for the first time to have a serious discussion away from their clans when the news item and their aggressor rudely interrupted them. They ran outside to continue their discussion.

Flunky: "This news item is just confirming what I was telling you. I am moving out with half of my clan."

Redd: "I don't think that's the best thing to do. Man is very dirty and no matter how clean they pretend to be or want to be, you can still find food for your clan."

Flunky: "You do not understand Redd, things have not been easy for us over the past six months. Our birth rate is very high, and in spite of the death rate, our population is growing at an alarming rate."

Redd: "Don't insult me Flunky. You know it is the same thing with us. Next, you will be telling me that the economic crisis has sent out more scavengers and now you have to share your garbage with some men."

Flunky: "Maybe Redd, but you house rats will always have food because you eat everything. We are more selective. We prefer garbage."

Redd laughed, "shi-shi shi-shi," before replying: "You can turn into house rats."

Flunky: "And change our style of living? No way!"

Redd: "But where will you go?"

Flunky: "I told you, I just came back from the Capital and the amount of garbage there is unbelievable. I can feed my family for months on end without any fear of scarcity."

Redd: "Yuk, how do the people stand so much garbage? Doesn't it stink?"

Flunky: "I guess, like us, they get used to it and don't smell it anymore. One finds a lot of garbage strewn all over the place almost at each fifty-meter interval or so. If the people want to pretend that it is outside their houses and so doesn't affect them, who am I to argue with them? They provide food for us."

Redd: "Wouldn't your move cause a war between you and the other rats in that vicinity?"

Flunky: "Not really. I met all their clan chiefs and we negotiated. There is enough for everyone."

Redd: "I'll miss you if ever you moved, Flunky. But I guess you have to do what is good for your clan."

Flunky: "I'll miss you too, Redd. But don't look so gloomy. I'll keep in touch and you can come and visit us when we settle."

Redd: "I guess so. But Flunky, what will you do if the Capital decides to emulate Aloh? Will you come back?"

Flunky: "I honestly don't know yet. I haven't thought that far ahead."

Redd: "You'll stop by to bid us farewell before you leave, won't you?"

Flunky: "You bet I will."

Redd: "You're okay for a field rat."

Flunky laughed, "shi shi-shi shi," and said: "You too, pal. See you."

They bade each other farewell just as the security lights were turned on and they scurried away in their different directions.

# Chapter Two

Four million field rats were assembled inside the Aloh municipal stadium in Bepanda. It was two days before the move, and Flunky had called a meeting for last minute instructions on the move to the Capital.

The time was three o'clock in the morning. This hour was chosen because it was the safest. It was too late for any hazards and too early for human disturbance. The rats covered almost all the space in the stadium. Had lights suddenly been turned on, it would have looked like a crowd of tiny spectators at a football match.

Flunky stood in the middle of the stadium flanked by forty of his chosen generals. He looked around and sat on his hind legs to see and be seen. The shi-shi shi-shi and shu-shu shu-shu immediately stopped and Flunky addressed the assembly.

"My dear brothers and sisters," he began, "you are all here today because you have accepted that the move to the Capital is the best thing to do. The Capital for us right now is the 'Promised Land'. However, we cannot all move. Only those who want to go should do so. Again, not all those who would like to go can make it because the journey will not be without hazards. For those who want to go but are afraid of the difficulties they will encounter, let me tell them that the sunshine at the end of the tunnel should be their vision. I would, however, counsel that pregnant rats, parents with babies of tender age, the aged and those not physically fit to attempt the journey, should not go. The final decision rests with each and every one of you. It is never a happy occasion when we have to leave friends and family. For those

7

who are staying, console yourselves with the thought that the fewer you are, the more food you will have. For those who are leaving, remember that 'nothing ventured, nothing gained'.

"Now for the strategy, we cannot all travel in one group. Those who want to go will assemble at the old airport on Thursday at nine p.m. You will be divided into groups of one hundred thousand. A general, who will be assisted by ten lieutenants, will head each group. Any questions or suggestions?" Flunky asked. He paused, looked around and said, "Yes?" pointing to a rat that had a question.

"If we see other places we think we can live in, is it okay for us to stay, or do all of us have to get to the Capital?"

"Thanks for asking the question," Flunky replied. "We are first of all individuals who make up family units. It would be good for many of us to stick together. But I think it's okay for any of you to stop on the way if you see other towns you find more lucrative. Actually, there are many towns on the way and any group of rats can decide to live in any. Except someone has any objections, I think the only thing we would appreciate is that you let your group general or any of his lieutenants know of your decision so that we can account for everyone when we get to the Capital. Any more questions?"

"If one gets tired, what should one do?" one rat asked.

"I think if anyone gets too tired to keep pace with his or her group, he or she is free to rest and wait for the next group. Anyone else with something to say?"

No one had any other question or comment, so Flunky continued: "We leave on Thursday at two-hourly intervals. The general leads his group. After every thousand rats, the lieutenant leads. Move abreast in six lines and make as little noise as possible. Cover as much distance as possible during the night, then rest during the day and eat whatever you can find. But please, do not wander far off from the group.

In all circumstances, no one should leave the group alone. Stay together as much as possible at all times."

He took a pause to drink some water before continuing. "The journey is long. It could take anywhere between five days and a week. Barring any eventualities, we should all be in the Capital next weekend. If any unforeseen difficulties arise on the way the general and his lieutenants are responsible for taking a decision. My dear brothers and sisters, the journey will be worth it when we reach the Capital. We should disperse now as quietly as we can and return to our respective homes. Thank you all for coming."

The meeting had lasted exactly one hour and might have been a non-event except for a little incident that happened to Ben Mbaku as the rats were leaving the stadium.

Ben was a forty-five-year-old journalist, married, with five children and usually drank too much. He was a brilliant journalist who would have been sacked many times over because of his drinking problem. What usually saved him was the simple fact that no matter how drunk or insulting he was to his boss and colleagues, the sight of a microphone immediately cleared his brain and transformed him into one of the most impressive journalists the country had. At many meetings to decide his fate, it was generally agreed that he was a '*soûlard capable*', and so he was allowed to continue working.

That morning, Ben had gotten up and taken his breakfast of coffee. When his wife reminded him of the children's school fees, he told her that he had no money. He went to work, finished his shift, and went straight to the finance service to ask for a salary advance, supposedly to pay his children's school fees. One hour later, at 3 p.m. to be exact, Ben was already drinking beer and discussing politics with friends in one of his famous watering joints. He never even noticed when old friends left and new ones took over. He continued drinking and buying drinks for his friends. When he became too rowdy, the hostess of the bar asked him very firmly to leave.

Already drunk, Ben left the first bar for the second. As he got in, he spotted an old school friend and walked over to him. He recognised the other person drinking with the school friend as a priest. Then he started saying to the hearing of everyone, "Have priests no shame these days, F-a-ther? You come right into a bar and drink?" No one answered him, but he continued anyway, "What about Stephen's wife whom you are going out with? Father, I thought you are married to God?"

Feeling very embarrassed and knowing that Ben, in that mood, would only stop if they left, the school friend and the priest decided to leave the bar. Ben followed them outside as he continued to abuse the priest. Totally confused and embarrassed, the priest took out his car keys and was trying to open someone else's car when Ben said, "Father, have you graduated from stealing people's wives to stealing people's cars?"

At 2 a.m. when the bar was closing, Ben was asked to leave. He was already totally drunk and incoherent. When he left the bar, the cold night air hit him and he felt like peeing. Unable to unzip his trousers, he let nature take its course as he urinated in his pants. Ben staggered on to the road, singing a popular song with the slur of a drunk. He watched cars passing by as his vision saw double and triple lights. He needed a taxi to get home so he tried stopping a taxi but could not even remember his destination. Instead, the taxi drivers got angry with Ben for wasting their time and called him names before taking off. Thus, he started the slow and painful journey of staggering in what he considered the general direction of his home.

Outside the stadium, too tired to continue, feeling sleepy and wanting to go to the toilet, he bent down, defecated in his pants, fell on the grass and went to sleep.

Two hours later, the alcohol started wearing off as the cold air gradually seeped into Ben's clothes. He turned on his side and went back to sleep.

The rats came out of the stadium, not all of them taking to Flunky's advice to go home. They decided to linger around and look for food while playing. Coming upon Ben who smelled a cocktail of alcohol, faeces and urine, the rats thought they had found a bonanza.

A few minutes after Ben had turned over and gone to sleep again, he felt many tiny hands caressing his body. He was beginning to have erotic dreams when he felt pain on his chest, his arms and his legs. The pain cleared his head faster than a dose of cold water or the microphone would have done. He opened his eyes slowly and saw hundreds of tiny creatures all over his body. He could not immediately tell what they were. For a moment he was paralysed with fear as he imagined he had died and was seeing his own ghost. He looked around tentatively but couldn't make out where the half-light of pre-dawn was. As his eyes became used to the darkness and he could decipher the "shi-shi" of the rats and recognised what they were, he screamed so loud that the rats were frightened. That is when he became aware of the fact that the rats were in his pants and all over his body. He looked around him and saw hundreds of rats all over the place. He had to be hallucinating. This many rats could not be in one place at the same time. Afraid that he would end up dead if he were not already, he knelt down and started praying:

"Lord, please take away these creatures from me and I promise I will never sin again. Lord, save me from these monsters and I will never touch a drink as long as I live. God, I promise to be a good father. I promise to take care of my wife and children. Lord, I promise never to ridicule anyone again. I promise never to repeat gossips about priests. Lord, I promise to go to Church every Sunday and to be a good Christian. God, I promise to keep all these promises if only you take these creatures away. I ask you all these through Christ our Lord, Amen."

When he finished praying, he lifted his head, looked around him and there were no more rats. He could not tell if the rats had been a figment of his imagination or not. But he intended to keep the promises he had made.

He got up from the ground and started walking home. Dawn was fast approaching, and there were people already going about their businesses. Ben would have liked to take one of the cabs that were now running in the early hours of the morning, but he could smell himself. He did not think any taxi would (carry him smelling the way he did. Besides, the walk would do him some good because he needed to think. As Ben walked by the front of a closed glass shop, he saw a reflection of a dirty-looking bagman. He stopped, looked around to see who it could be and realised that he was the only person standing outside the store. He saw an old man with a torn shirt and tattered trousers. His hair was unkempt. What had happened to the young man who had left the school of journalism with the world at his feet, bubbling with "the star is the limit" attitude? Where had that man gone?

"My God," Ben thought, "I am a father, a husband and someone whom people respect. No, not I, but my voice." What had happened to the young girl he had married, the mother of his children? How long since he remembered that he had a wife! How could any woman love this reflection in the mirror? What kind of a father was he to his children? How did his children feel about him? Were they proud of the journalist and hateful of the father? How did one make up for being a part-time father? How many times had he stayed out all night? How did his wife see him and why had she tolerated the abuse all these years? How could he make it better for his wife and children? What about his friends and colleagues?

As if in slow motion, Ben recalled all the times he had abused other people because he himself was feeling angry at the system. How was he going to overcome all the stress and pressures of life that had pushed him to start drinking in the first place? And where was he to go from there?

He was still standing in front of the store shocked by his reflection when someone walked by him, covered his nostrils and crossed to the other side of the road. That reminded Ben of the other thing which the store glass could not pick up - the stench from his body. Ben hurried home, wondering if he still had a home and a family waiting for him.

When he got home, his wife, who was now used to what others referred to as her curse, quietly ran a hot bath, put in the last of her bath foam and helped Ben to undress and bathe. In her mind she was already seeing herself going to work late and the children being late for school if she had to wash Ben before going to get the children ready for school and make sure that everyone had eaten. Ben surprised her by offering and insisting on washing his soiled clothes. After that, he asked her to call his office and tell them that he was sick. The second part really scared her because Ben was never one to be absent from work because of a minor thing as a hangover.

"Are you sick?" she asked.

"A little. But more than anything, I need time to rest and sort out a few things. Can I have a heavy breakfast later?"

"Sure, but do you mean you really want a heavy breakfast?"

"Of course, yes! Is there something wrong with your hearing?"

"Well, you can understand if I am surprised that you want breakfast. That's all."

"Then you are in for lots of surprises because a few things are going to change around here."

"If you say so," Meg answered with some scepticism. She left to carry out his request and to prepare the children for school. Throughout that morning, she wondered what it was that kept her married to the man she called her husband. Her oldest daughter looked at her with angry eyes as if to echo her mother's thoughts, but her mother shook her head, telling her as she often did, that it was neither the time nor the place.

After the children had left for school, Meg got to the room to find that her husband had finished bathing, but instead of washing his clothes, he had wrapped them up and thrown them into the garbage.

Meg made breakfast of pancakes, scrambled eggs and coffee, placed them on a tray and took it to her husband. She found him running a slight temperature. Ben dug into the breakfast with relish but was able to eat only a few bites before vomiting everything.

Using a napkin to clean his mouth, Ben said, "I'm sorry." Meg jumped. She was getting nervous. Her husband was acting very strange. Ben, apologising to her? She could not remember the last time he did that.

"Would you like to go to the hospital?" Meg asked.

"I guess so. Look for my medical booklet and please do get my vaccination card too," Ben replied.

"Ben, you are scaring me. What is it? I noticed small bites on your body. What happened?"

In answer, Ben bent his head and looked sheepish. Meg gave up and went to look for the booklet and card.

Ben was in a dilemma. How would he tell his wife that rats attacked him and that he risked having rabies or some other poisonous infection? Would she believe him? Ben bent his head and remembered the money he had taken from his office for the children's fees. What had happened to it? "My God," Ben shuddered, "I have become someone whom even I do not like."

Rats, like cats, dogs, or some other domestic animals, carry germs in their saliva or teeth that can transmit diseases when they bite a human being. Ben wondered if one or more of the rats that had bitten him were infected with some disease. He remembered a case he had covered of a patient who had been bitten by a dog that had rabies and towards the end, the man had been foaming at the mouth and barking like a dog. Ben shivered at the thought of an early demise. He owned one small house in the village that he had built during the early days of his career before the stress of his job turned him into a drunk. He had some money which his organisation owed him although it was not much. But if he died, what would become of his wife and children? What was he going to leave for them? "What a parent I have turned out to be!" Ben muttered. He got up and turned to the only other solace he knew besides the contents of the bottle: the Bible.

When Meg returned and found Ben holding the Bible, she was so scared that she immediately asked, "Ben, you are not planning to die, are you?"

"What makes you say that?"

"You have been behaving very strangely since you came in this morning."

"I have not been much of a husband to you, nor much of a parent to the children, have I?"

"Now you are really scaring me."

"How have you stood me all these years, Meg? How did I get so lucky?"

"I married you for love, 'until death do us part.' Remember? Stop being churlish and let's go to the hospital."

\*\*\*

Ben was a lucky person. While covering a vaccination campaign a few months back, Ben had also queued up to be given an anti tetanus vaccine, which now helped to protect him from any bacteria he could have contracted from the rats. After running a couple of tests, the doctor found nothing wrong with Ben. But he decided to prescribe some antibiotics for him and to keep him in the hospital for a few days of observation.

Meg was not told what was going on. Ben asked the doctor to keep it a secret, so Meg never knew what had happened to Ben. When his family visited him, Ben had changed so positively that even the children prayed he stayed that way.

Ben was surprised at the number of people who came to visit him at the hospital. His colleagues, friends and other family members brought him food, money, flowers and cards. It suddenly dawned on Ben that people loved him in spite of his rude and unkind lifestyle. If they loved him the way he was, then they would love him more if they found him a changed person. Ben silently promised God that he would change and be a better person.

He was kept in hospital for a week. Meg worried about the bills, but somehow, whenever they needed money to buy drugs, there was money. Meg had borrowed money to pay the hospital bills on the day Ben was supposed to be discharged. But to her surprise, when she got to the hospital the bills had been paid and Ben gave her an extra hundred thousand francs to keep. There were tears in Meg's eyes when Ben told her where the money had come from. The tears were not only for the kindness people had shown them but also for the fact that Ben had given her the money to keep. After so many years a miracle had happened and she was going to get back the Ben she had fallen in love with and married. She silently thanked whatever deity had transformed her husband.

\*\*\*

The first group of rats left Aloh on Thursday as scheduled. The first hurdle occurred at the outskirts of Aloh, about two kilometres from the airport. The rats got to the banks of an old stream that had become a pile of smelly and slimy mud, more treacherous than quicksand. The first hundred or so rats entered the mud and got stuck and could neither move backwards nor forwards. The first lieutenant called a halt and asked the others closest to the incident to see if they could find sticks that were long enough to enable the rats to come out of the mud.

The combined sound of the multitude of sinking rats making their last "shwi-shwi, shui-shui, shwii-shwii" was so heart-breaking that other rats would have gone into the mud in a desperate effort to save their comrades. But fortunately, the general arrived the scene, took the situation in hand and declared that any such move will only result in more rats getting killed. Some rats were so discouraged that they decided to return to Aloh.

The general called his lieutenants together and held a little conference. After a heated debate, there was a consensus that a detour be made. The rats were to keep as close to the main road as possible, but stay on the edges in order to avoid being run over by cars. The message was passed on and repeated along the line. Twenty rats were left behind to wait for the next battalion of rats to pass on the message. This procedure would be repeated with each battalion until all the rats became aware of the detour.

At a halfway point where the rats were supposed to rest longer, some rats decided to remain there while the others continued on their way. The greatest calamity would occur three hours later. While resting during the day as previously arranged, the rats were asleep and unaware of ongoing road repairs, which resulted in the collision of vehicles that somersaulted and fell on the sleeping, unsuspecting rats, killing over five hundred of them and injuring many.

***

The courier rat is the smallest in the rat family. It has a longer mouth, very tiny limbs, can run very fast and needs very little food to sustain itself. It is not very choosy about what it eats but generally prefers dry food such as paper and wood. It generally lives in warehouses from where it visits other rats or is met at specific places to be given oral messages which it listens to and disseminates to various destinations. Due to its mobility, the courier rat does not breed as much as the other rat families. In order to facilitate its job and run it with some efficiency, the courier rat has special routes assigned to it by its clan head.

One message is given to several rats travelling the same route. Rats plying the same routes never jump on to the same vehicles, so that in case of an accident or other untimely deaths, the message still gets delivered. They listen attentively to the messages and when they get to their destinations, the messages are transmitted to the recipients.

When Flunky got to the Capital, he immediately contacted some courier rats that could take messages to and from Aloh. The first message he sent was a short one:

Capital, 15 December.

Dear Redd,

I'm sending you this letter by a courier rat that I met. They are in a hurry because the goods they want to accompany are due to leave any time. The first two of my teams arrived here. There were a few casualties but that was to be expected. We arrived hungry and worn out but the sight of all the garbage we found lifted many spirits. Everyone is settling down fine. I'll keep you informed. I

miss you already. Do give my regards to your family.
Sincerely yours,
Flunky.

Aloh, 20 December.

Dear Flunky,
Thank you for your last letter. It was a relief to hear from you. I am happy you arrived safely. I am sure by now more of your clan have arrived. Aloh is booming with preparations for Christmas. There is more food than ever. However, we had a real scare because one of the babies ate our hostess' new dress. She was so angry that she got a trap and some rat poison. I lost about fifty of the younger rats that had not yet been trained in ways of detecting traps. We had to stay holed up for three days but everything is fine now. I will have to prepare lessons for the younger generations. I think we will live peacefully if we leave women's dresses alone because they are usually very particular about those things.

How is the Capital? Still up to your expectations? Well, take care. Hard to believe this, but I do miss you.
My warmest regards,
Redd.

# Chapter Three

Mamie Nyanga had been part of the household for as long as Sue could remember. Sue first noticed her about two weeks after she moved into her house. She had been relaxing, watching television alone at about 8 p.m. when she noticed a rat come out from the direction of the kitchen and walk very slowly, "koonya, koonya, koonya, koonya," moving one step after the other in all majesty, as if she was a model walking down the runway. The rat took all her time until she came to the middle of the carpet and sat there as if she had all the right in the world to be there.

The rat was different from most other rats because its fur was a lighter brown and had a patch of white on its forehead and tail. Sue was so mesmerised by the audacity of this rat that by the time she got up to hit it, it had disappeared. The first day set a pattern for the rest of the days. The rat spent her days in the kitchen, eating whatever it could and then coming out to the living room in the evenings in the same majestic manner. After numerous attempts to kill the rat, with many bumps into the furniture and many scrapes on the knee, Sue decided to leave the rat alone and named it Mamie Nyanga.

Mamie Nyanga's presence in Sue's living room became so normal that when Sue was alone with her, she held a one-sided conversation with Mamie Nyanga in which she recounted her day's ups-and-downs as a young beautiful journalist in the Capital. Sue became so used to Mamie Nyanga's presence that when she was not at home, she would time-set the television to come on automatically.

21

During the rare times that Mamie Nyanga failed to appear when Sue was at home, she would miss her to the extent of wanting to search for her.

Mamie Nyanga had sustained all the other rats that had come into Sue's house, not only because of the uneasy truce between Sue and her, but also for the simple reason that she now mastered Sue's routine. Sue normally left her house at 8 a.m. and Mamie Nyanga knew she could then roam the house at will. But she otherwise stayed in the kitchen cupboard, where she nibbled on anything from bread and paper to groundnuts. After she had had her fill, she would run around the house making "shwi-shwi, shwi-shwi," and that would be the signal for other rats to come and feast. At twelve-thirty, as soon as they heard the key in the lock, they would all scurry into the nearest hole to wait for Sue to come in, eat, sleep and return to work later. At night when Sue was asleep, most of the rats came out again to take food and hoard in their holes.

*** 

In most houses, garbage was generally accumulated during the day, taken out at night and thrown out somewhere in the streets where it was expected that the City Council would have the courtesy of disposing of it. In the Capital, this service is either neglected or does not exist. Eventually, garbage piles up and emits a horrible stench. Each person approaching the garbage dump usually has his or her hands over his nostrils, and to avoid stepping on any garbage, stands far away to empty refuse. Sometimes it lands on the heap and at other times it starts a new heap. Under these circumstances, it has become the norm to fill up half a street with garbage. Roundabouts have been known to be made up of a mountain of garbage so high that vehicles passing on one side cannot be seen by those on the opposite side.

May happened to be in Sue's house that day by accident. They had met three weeks earlier at the Ministry of Public Service where they had both gone to follow-up their files. Having lost contact with each other for over five years, exclamations of 'eh!s' 'ah!s' and 'oh!s' were many.

"How long are you going to be in town?" Sue asked.

"I'm going back tomorrow."

"Oh, no! I would have loved us to spend sometime together, and do some catching up."

"Me, too. But I have to leave with my brother-in-law in the morning. I'll be back here in three weeks. How do I get in touch with you then?"

"Easy! Either meet me at the office or come straight home. You'll stay with me, won't you?"

"You forget I don't know where you live, and neither do I know this city well."

"No problem. The house is easy to find. Take a taxi to Grace Pharmacy. Make a right turn in front of the pharmacy, after the second garbage dump, make another right turn, and a few metres away you will see a house with a blue fence on the left. That's it."

"Then the next time I visit, I will come and stay with you."

"Good. I am looking forward to your visit."

That was three weeks ago and last night May had found the house easily. The following morning Sue went to work and May got up to make breakfast at the same time that Mamie Nyanga was getting out for hers. They met at the kitchen doorway. Momentarily stunned at finding someone in the house at that hour on a weekday, Mamie Nyanga lost her usual advantage over an adversary and that gave May the opportunity to pick up a broom, hit her with it, pick her up and throw her into the garbage. A few hours later, she took the garbage out in plain daylight and dumped it at the first garbage heap she found.

That is where Flunky and a few other rats collecting food for storage found the wounded-but-not-yet-dead Mamie Nyanga and carried her into their hole. That night, and for the next two nights, Sue came home too tired to notice Mamie Nyanga's absence. The added distraction of having a friend in the house made Mamie Nyanga's absence to be noticed only two days after May had left, and that was already a week after her actual disappearance.

Sue felt as if she had lost a dear friend. What could have happened to Mamie Nyanga? Could she have gone out and lost her way? Sue knew that she never contributed her money to the Pesticide Company because she had refused to play God with the life of any of His creatures. "Oh! What could have happened to my companion?" she kept asking herself during those hours when she sat and watched television alone. There was a vague memory of May mentioning something about a rat. Why hadn't she paid more attention?

# Chapter Four

N o one could have planned and executed the sequence of events that followed with the precision in which they actually happened. They led to the feeble attempt by the Mayor of the Capital to do something about the garbage situation in the city.

Twentieth October activities in the Capital were scheduled to be executed with clockwork precision because that is the one occasion the President personally attends. The ordinary invited guests to the grandstand (Tribunes A and C) were expected to arrive at 7.00 a.m., the diplomatic corps at 7.30 a.m., while government representatives were scheduled to arrive between 7.30 and 8.30 a.m. The Prime Minister would arrive at 8.45 a.m., the President of the National Assembly at 8.50 a.m. and the President at 9.00 a.m. prompt, after which celebrations would immediately start. No one was allowed near or around the grandstand after that.

The Minister of Women's and Social Affairs left her "Denver" residence to make the usual thirty minutes' drive to the celebration grounds, with five minutes to spare. She had not counted on any traffic jam in a town which normally had little traffic during public holidays.

Ten minutes from her house, her car entered the major road, got into a lane and slowed down behind another car in front of it. Within ten minutes, there were cars behind her a quarter of a mile long. As the minutes turned to three, four, five, and then ten, she started sweating profusely. The air conditioner in her black Mercedes Benz 280 SEL was working all right, but if the traffic did not start to move soon, then she would be late for the ceremony.

The President had become quite intolerant about lateness to public ceremonies and her absence would be quite conspicuous and most annoying because she was the only female member of Government. In desperation, she asked her driver to try and manoeuvre the car out of the lane, but it was impossible as cars were now jammed bumper to bumper, and were over a mile long.

Totally frustrated and close to tears, she asked her gendarme bodyguard to go out and find out what was causing the traffic jam and see if he could do something about it. Her bodyguard got out, walked for about five minutes, came back and reported that there was a traffic bottleneck further down the road where a garbage dump had blocked the street. The garbage had made it impossible for two cars at a time to occupy the narrow street.

At nine o'clock, hopeless and dejected, knowing she dare not continue to the ceremonial grounds even if the traffic jam cleared, the Minister got out of her car in an attempt to walk home and call the police. A second later, she wished she had remained in the car. As soon as people recognised her, they started booing and insulting her.

"Health for all by the year 2000!"

*"Voleuse."*

"What do you do with our taxes?"

"Is this the legacy we are leaving for our children?"

"Ill-health for all by the year 2000!"

*"Man no run."*

Some people openly laughed at her while others used four-letter words. "It does not only happen to others," they shouted. There was nothing her bodyguard could do except watch in helpless resignation.

She had two choices - either to go back and sit in her car and risk being lynched for being part of the administration that was causing disorder or walk back to her house in a rain of insults. She had an even bigger problem of explaining her absence to the President.

\*\*\*

The Mayor's wife had spent two weeks and a fortune in Paris choosing the dress she wanted to wear to the Twentieth October gala at the Presidency. When she modelled the ivory-coloured Christian Dior dress in a shop at Champs Elysées, she decided she would have it or nothing else. The dress clung to her fifty-year-old-well-kept-body, showing her figure to perfection. The dress matched her hair which was starting to grey, and added lustre to her chocolat-au-lait complexion. After paying for shoes, a handbag and earrings to match, she was satisfied with her purchase.

On that evening of the gala at the Presidency, she had a warm bath, coifed her hair and looked gorgeous in special lingerie she had bought for the occasion. It was now time to wear the "knock them dead" dress. She reached into the closet, took out the dress and screamed so loud that her husband ran out naked from the bathroom.

"What is it, honey?"

Too shocked to speak, she pointed to her dress, carelessly thrown on the bed.

"What, honey? You scared me half to death."

"Rats have eaten holes into my dress."

"God, honey! Is that all? You can wear another dress."

"No, I cannot. I won't go to the gala."

"Are you mad? What would the President say?"

"I don't care. I've had it right up here with rats in this city."

"But, honey, you know the President will notice your absence."

"No, he won't. There will be too many people there for him to notice. I don't want to wear anything else."

"*Cherie*, please, do you want me to lose my job? You know that even if he doesn't notice your absence, his pinions will tell him. The man is so paranoid these days that he cannot even tell the difference between friend and foe."

27

The mayor held his wife in his arms and pleaded with her to wear another dress and attend the gala; but she was adamant. She would not attend the Presidential gala.

# Chapter Five

Any Mayor usually presides at a civil status wedding in the Capital City. In this case, the senior Mayor was presiding at this particular ceremony because it was the wedding of a princess of the soil to the son of a multi-millionaire arms merchant. A friend to both families, he was doing them the honour of celebrating the civil part of their wedding, in the same way that the Archbishop would be the one to perform the church rites later on in the day with eight priests.

The ceremonial hall was packed to capacity. Everybody who was somebody in the Capital City was there, including the media. All the TV cameras were focused on the couple. It was now the most solemn part of the ceremony, the part where after the exchange of rings the Mayor was about to take the hands of the couple, place them in his and say, "By the powers invested in me," and this is when something strange happened.

The Mayor never got to "I now pronounce you husband and wife." If he did, no one heard. There was first, snickering, then all-out shouting as the spell-bound audience watched with fascination a small rat leave the Mayor's coat pocket and crawl slowly up his shoulder.

Cameramen had a field day. Close-ups of the rat and the Mayor's embarrassed face were taken and later shown on national television with questions and commentaries that the state could no longer refuse to face.

The nation could not believe that a tiny rat could have caused such a national furore as to force the City Council, government representatives and the public at large to sit down and have a mini-national conference on the garbage situation or non-existence of sanitary measures in the Capital City.

The Mayor's wife, whose relationship with her husband had been at the best quite cold since the incident of the Twentieth of October, watched with fear as her husband aged ten more years before her very own eyes within a few days.

"*Cherie*, please resign. Don't let this affair kill you," she pleaded.

"I can't. That will mean accepting defeat."

"Honey, I hate to say this, but you are already defeated. Besides, you have given a deaf ear to the people's problems for too long."

"If I'm given another chance, I'll try to make amends."

"Haven't you had enough time to do that? Do the honourable thing and resign. Even the President cannot perform a miracle on this."

"My dear, resigning will not do. I still have to finish my term. Listen to all the insinuations the media are making. If I leave without cleaning things up, the garbage that a commission of inquiry will dig up, will stink worse than what's in the city at the moment."

"So what? We can go and live in France."

"You mean run away? You know that I cannot live in France. I hate the place. Besides, he who runs away from a problem only postpones it."

"Would you rather die from all the tension, be disgraced or even end up in prison?"

"Honey, look here, stop worrying. I'll go and see Pa. I'm sure he can do something."

The wife knew exactly who the "Pa" was. It was the old native doctor on whom her husband spent huge amounts of money for everything concerning his life. They had had many arguments on the issue of serving God and man, and agreed to disagree on the issue. There was no way she could make her husband see that his blessings came from God and no one else. But she decided not to argue too much, otherwise the native doctor would concoct some story of her being the "bad luck" to her husband. The irony was that her husband would believe the "Pa" rather than her. So she decided to avoid the issue.

But how could she make her husband understand that the "Pa" would be watching television too and listening to the radio and was probably expecting him to come and bring huge sums of money for the magic ritual to keep him in office? She looked at her husband sadly and the echoes of a famous poem came to her mind:

Oh frail man!
Can he really forget?
That the higher he climbs
The deadlier he falls?
Can one make faeces
On his way in
And not meet maggots
On his way out?

# Chapter Six

Flunky heard about the mounting tension in the city and the likely outcome while he was tending to Mamie Nyanga. He had fallen in love with her. He could not afford to leave her with her ribs still broken and patched up. But like a good general, he knew where duty lay.

He summoned a meeting of all the clan heads and their advisers at the Lycée Bilingue football field at 2 a.m.

After Flunky's welcome address he handed over the floor to the oldest inhabitant of the city. He had been chief before Flunky and had chosen Flunky to replace him when he went on retirement.

"I have lived to a ripe old age and will now probably die only of natural causes because I have been able to gauge man's tempo and direction in this city," the chief rat said. "The furore is now higher than I have ever witnessed. So I assume that the retaliation will be swifter, faster, and more deadly than anything we have experienced before."

"Just what sort of reprisals can we expect?" a rat asked.

"For a start, the sales of pesticides will increase because people will try to kill as many of us as possible. Then I expect that before the Council can mobilise finances and services to carry away garbage, attempts will be made to reduce the quantity of garbage by burning it. I hope you have all undertaken drills in your constituencies on pesticide detection, and what to do when you smell smoke."

"How soon can we expect some of these measures?" one rat asked.

Flunky took over again and said: "First, I think we should store as much food as possible within the next few days.

Now, more than ever, we have to be more cautious and vigilant."

The old rat took the floor again: "We do not know for how long we may have to stay undercover this time. So I advise that when the time comes to go underground the hoarded food be rationed very carefully. My bones are too old and tired now. I may not be with you in the next council meeting, so I'd like to wish you all good luck now."

"Grandpa, do you think any move the people make is likely to be a permanent one?" a small rat asked.

"I would hardly think so. I have seen so many of these feeble bursts of attempts to keep this city clean die out before they are executed. Except some drastic changes are made, the pattern will remain the same. However, I will advise that you keep your eyes and ears open."

"Does anyone have anymore questions or suggestions?" Flunky asked as he looked around. No one said anything, so he adjourned the meeting by asking every rat to continue thinking about the pending problem and consider alternative ways of solving it.

# Chapter Seven

S ue needed time to think. She did not like sitting in her office to do so. She had been assigned to do a human-interest story on the occasion of Labour Day on the first of May. Many ideas ran through her head but she had nothing fixed. Sometimes it paid to walk around and think. Sue left her office and walked down to the meeting room.

The meeting room of the National Radio and Television centre was a large room on the second floor of the building where journalists met to do various things, ranging from work plans to holding meetings. It was also the biggest room in the building where journalists came to relax, discuss or gossip. The meeting room was built to house a bar and a cafeteria in which most journalists spent their time. It was there that most friendships as well as enmities were made.

The meeting room or watering hole had a character of its own. There was never a quiet moment in the room except on those rare occasions when an official meeting was held there. As Sue entered the room she stopped and listened to the conversation, searching for a group to join. The chairs and tables in the meeting room were arranged according to the desires and number of people who wanted to sit together. There was a group of older journalists standing at the counter near the bar, discussing the new cabinet reshuffle and what it meant to the economy of the state. Sue could barely pick up a few words here and there. At the farther end of the hall usually called the "quiet corner" was a group of younger journalists drinking beer and looking very serious over whatever it was they were planning. This was supposed to be the "fourth estate", Sue thought, yet they did not come close to it.

"I wonder what I ever saw in this profession. yeah, Ben and the other voices I heard over the radio," Sue's thoughts ran. If only people knew that the glamour and hype which the media as a whole was reputed to have was just a farce, especially in this small African country where journalists were useful only if they toed the government line and reported what they were asked to say!

Thinking about Ben brought a smile to Sue's face. He had turned out to be a letdown. But she was happy for the Ben she had seen at the hospital and prayed that somehow he could get off alcohol and pick up the pieces of his life again.

There was silence the first time Ben entered the meeting room after leaving hospital. Rumour already had it that Ben had quit drinking. Someone greeted him and asked, "How about a beer to celebrate your recovery, Ben?"

"Thanks, Mark, but I beg to pass," Ben answered in good humour, then quipped, "The doctor has asked me to lay off the stuff."

"Is that for real, Ben?" someone asked.

"I'm afraid so, buddy."

"Well, it's just a matter of time, isn't it?" Mark said as some people started edging towards the door, not wanting to witness what they thought would be a fight with Ben.

But they stopped when Ben answered good naturedly, "As a matter of fact, I will need all of you to help me stay off the poison for good." Then seeing that he had everyone's attention, Ben continued, "I would like to apologise to those that I have insulted and those I have hurt unnecessarily during my inhibited moments. I would like to take this opportunity too to thank all those who came to visit me at the hospital. Thank you too for the gifts of yourselves, presents, and all." There were tears in Ben's eyes as he ended. Someone started clapping, and before long everyone was clapping and people were hugging Ben.

Sue was in the hall that day. For her, it was a very special moment. Ben's voice over the radio had been the reason she had gone into journalism, but her disappointment at the real Ben and the dream-one had been so great that she had started reconsidering her career. Ben had been a good mentor to her when he was sober, and sometimes she had been Ben's conscience, for she was the only young journalist who had the guts to tell Ben to his face what she thought of him. Sue was the first to hug Ben spontaneously and say, "Welcome back, big brother."

"From where, little sister?" Ben joked.

"From whatever it was that had dragged you down," Sue answered.

"Well, if this is what being sick does to you, then maybe you should get sick more often, Ben," another colleague said.

Two weeks later, Ben and Sue were assigned to cover the national mini-conference. Ben had not been sent to cover any event outside the studio for years. The new assignment was a validation of his sober state.

\*\*\*

The first day of the mini-conference was a total disaster. The Mayor got up to speak amidst boos. His well-prepared and properly rehearsed speech about the responsibilities of everyone vis-à-vis the garbage situation was never heard. The participants had come to the conference in camps. Members of the pro-Mayor group shouted down the leader of a group that came to turn the conference into an "accountability-of-how-the-municipality-funds-were-used". The champion of the "keep our Capital clean" tried to bring the meeting on course. He received no better treatment and the day closed without any opening. When the whole spectacle was shown on television that night, the assembly resembled a crowd of school children let loose in a classroom without a teacher.

The next day, the presence of the Archbishop of the diocese of the Capital who the exasperated Mayor had invited after the previous day's debacle brought some order to the proceedings.

As the conference participants took their time over the deliberations, garbage continued to pile high in all the nooks and crannies of the city. The rats had a field day. They worked frantically, day and night, hoarding food.

*** 

To the delight of Flunky who was falling more and more in love by the day, Mamie Nyanga was slowly recovering. He knew she was a house rat and his only fear was whether he could turn her into a field rat and keep her by his side forever. She had been with them for over three weeks and if she could eat whatever they ate during that time, there was just a tiny chance that she could be convinced to stay forever. If not, he was willing to share half of his time between the field and the house.

After a very tiring night, Flunky got up early the next morning to send the following message to Redd:

Dear Redd,
Thank you very much for your last message. I know you must be worried about us. No! We are not planning on moving again. I believe that we will still be able to survive here even if the Capital City follows Aloh's example and endeavours to uphold sanitation. The time between when garbage is emptied and when it is picked up will be enough for us to gather food. We cannot continue to split or move on every time there is a threat to our existence. Besides, grandpa assures us that the efforts this time will be no

different from previous ones. Would you believe it? I am in love with a house rat. Did I have to fall in love with a house rat? I am scared that when she gets well she may not want to stay with me. I might turn into a house rat after all. Oh! Did I tell you about the bruised rat we picked up from the garbage?

How is everyone? Give my love to all your family.

Yours sincerely,

Flunky.

# Chapter Eight

The conference started the next day at 9 a.m. There was general quiet as each individual's shame of the previous day's debacle was reflected in the eyes of their neighbour. To cap it all, the Archbishop came in to chair the meeting ten minutes after everybody was seated. He began the meeting with a prayer:

"Lord, our heavenly Father, thank you for taking everyone home yesterday and for bringing them back here today to work together. We hope to find a solution to our general garbage situation in this city. Lord, you said that when two or more people are gathered in your name, you will be in their midst. Lend us your presence, dear Father. Guide and lead us as we seek solutions to our common problems. Give us tolerance so that we may be able to listen to each other. Open our hearts and minds so that we may think objectively. Help us put personal differences aside and work for the greater good of the city. Let us now say the Lord's Prayer together."

After the opening prayer, the Archbishop sat down and said, "Before we get into the heart of the matter at hand I propose that we make ground rules to respect during all sessions. We should all make the rules together, since they will be binding on all of us."

The general assembly accepted the Archbishop's proposal and the following rules were adopted:

1. Sessions shall start on time.
2. Members shall speak one at a time.
3. Listen attentively.
4. Respect each other.
5. Avoid repeating what has already been said.

6. Do not interrupt someone when they are still speaking.

The Archbishop took the floor again. "We have written the ground rules on the board. They will stay there everyday during all sessions and when in need, please do refer to them. Good! Can we begin? Anyone wishing to express his or her opinion should indicate by a show of the hand."

1st Speaker: I would propose that before we get into the matter at hand, the Mayor's office should let us know approximately what its annual income is and how that income is spent, in order to allow us know how to include our projected expenditure into the budget.

2nd Speaker: I don't think knowing the municipality's income is necessary at this stage. Trying to carry out an audit now will only cause unnecessary delays.

1st Speaker: I did not suggest an audit. A simple balance sheet would be fine.

Mayor: The Council is prepared to do whatever this conference proposes.

3rd Speaker: If I come up with a plan of action for this meeting, I would like to hope that unlike previous efforts, this one would keep our city clean forever. So I agree with the first speaker that an idea of the city's income is relevant.

"Excuse me..."

"I want to say..."

"Can I propose..."

Three speakers who had not been given the floor started speaking at the same time. The Archbishop had to hit the table and shout, "Ground rules," to bring the assembly back to order.

Calm returned and the meeting continued. "Yes?" the Archbishop went on.

4th Speaker: I know that we will sit here, talk and make plans that we believe are entirely feasible. The Council will promise to execute our proposals, and everybody will leave very happy. I have been part of this town for too long and I have lived through this spurt of energies. The question is, can the Council clean up our city? If so, for how long can the Council do so? I want to propose that each quarter take the responsibility of cleaning its area. Let's try that and see what happens.

5th Speaker: The Mayor and his Council have failed us too often. I propose that in order to solve our problem, we pass a vote of "no confidence" on the Mayor, conduct new elections and tackle this problem once and for all.

Mayor: I promise to do whatever is necessary to keep our city clean.

5th speaker: "You have fooled too many people too often."

4th Speaker: "I suggest that you tell that to your electorate."

Mayor: "But I have to finish my term, you don't have any quorum."

By this time, there was total disorder in the hall. It took some time for the Archbishop to restore calm again. Not succeeding very well, he called for a coffee break.

At the end of the week, the following was reported in the news:

"The week long conference on 'Keep our Capital clean' came to an end yesterday. The debate on what to do in order to keep our Capital clean was long and exhausting. After the fiasco of the first day, members of the conference settled down to serious business. It was generally agreed that the Council alone, with worn-out trucks and very few personnel, was inadequately equipped for the task. The services of a company, Rattles, have been hired to do the job. The question now on everyone's mind is for how long this endeavour will be maintained. Let's wait and see. This is Ben Mbaku reporting for the 8 p.m. news in the Capital city."

The above news item was heard over the radio and television pictures showed garbage heaps super-imposed on those of the brand new Renault trucks bought a few months ago by the Aloh Urban Council.

The news made headlines for several days. Many people received it with indifference, some with doubt, and the new comers to the city, with hope.

***

Flunky nibbled on a piece of stale bread under a cupboard and smiled at Mamie Nyanga as Sue and a friend discussed the likely outcome of the mini-national conference.

"Do you believe they will really manage to keep this place clean?"

"I sure hope so. Each time I travel out and come back to this lovely town, I feel really sick."

"Hmm. If they do succeed in removing all these garbage mounds, what would people use to give directions to their houses?"

Hearing this last statement, Flunky pushed away the piece of bread and muttered to Mamie Nyanga, "Gosh! What an irony! We are worried about what we will eat and how we will survive; they are worried about giving directions to their houses."

# Why the Cock is used
# for Sacrifice

It was pitch dark in the forest. The hunter squinted, trying to see well. But it was not possible. He cocked his ears attentively in order to listen to the sounds and sighs of the wind and of the inhabitants of the forest. Nothing. The hunter twitched his nostrils to smell the mixture of dung, leaves, and herbs as he tried to distinguish the smell of animals from those of the forest. He could smell nothing.

Fai came from a generation of hunters who had been trained through example and guidance to acquire the experience to differentiate between the sounds and smells of the forest. He could with assurance almost always identify the type of animal that was nearby just from its sound, smell, or movement.

He had been in the forest for two hours. But this particular day when he needed to catch the biggest animal he could for the sacrifice that awaited him in the village, all animals seemed to have gone on vacation or migrated to some other habitat. It was quite cold and Fai was well protected by the skins of lions he had killed. But in spite of the cold and heavy protection, he was sweating.

He was sixteen years old. Today was the most important day of his life in the village. The rites of passage for him and his age mates were a few days away and the highest initiation title will be given to the person who caught the most animals. The blood of the animals will be used for sacrifices to the gods while the meat will be shared to the villagers to be eaten. It was a festive season. Everyone waited for the occasion with excitement. The young men will be circumcised and prepared for passage into adulthood. The maidens in the village, together with the parents and the relatives of these youths, will all be watching out for who will get the highest title. Fai wanted the title so badly he could taste it in his mouth.

The young men of his age group in the village were twelve in number. Fai was at the tail end of the two-year age bracket, but he was by far the most ambitious and the strongest in his age group as he had proven on many occasions. The other young men will be in the forest too hunting for animals. They will bring back whichever animals they caught within the next three days. At the end of that time, they will be judged according to the number, size and quality of their catch. The fun was in the hunting, but for the villagers who only waited to eat, the game was what mattered.

Fai slowly let his breath out and offered a silent prayer to the gods of his clan. The gods could not let him down now. Then he heard a noise so slight that any one else would not have heard. He cocked his ears, twitched his nostrils and detected the sound of a leopard coming towards him. A leopard will be good. In fact, a leopard that day might just be what will tilt the scales in his favour. He was not supposed to know how the competition was going, but he still knew from the gossip in the village that it was quite keen. Fai squared his shoulders and waited for the leopard as the unsuspecting animal walked gracefully towards him. He said a little prayer to thank his gods, fired his gun and in a split second, the majestic animal sprang into the air as if to challenge him. It fell to the ground, refusing to show any signs of pain, and wagged its tail as if to congratulate the hunter. It took one last deep breath and died.

\*\*\*

That night, there was confusion in the forest. The animals had not faced this kind of threat before. From every corner of the forest came the wailing of pain and fear from the animals. By the time the competition came to an end a lot of animals would be killed.

Humans had always used animals for sacrifice whenever they had a problem with their gods. Today, all animals lived in perpetual fear of extinction. At ordinary times, man's taste for meat was enormous, but during sacrificial rituals, the need was even greater.

The lion, the king of the forest, called a meeting at a designated place on a certain day at a specific time to discuss this problem with all animals. The meeting took place in a clearing which resembled a stadium with a large stone standing in the middle. The top of the stone belonged to the lion, the king of the jungle, who would stand on it to address the other animals.

The snail knows that it is the slowest of all animals, so it left early for the meeting. The African giant land snail is enormous. Its shell is about 20 centimetres long and its body can measure up to 39 centimetres. It provides food to some natives and is also used for sacrifice. But because it is not as big as other animals, a lot of them have to be used for important sacrifices. It crawled gently on its belly, leaving a slimy residue on its path as it went along. On the way, the snail met the cock, which was busy playing and flapping its wings.

"Hi, cock."

"Hi, snail. Where are you going to?"

"Oh! I am going to the meeting. Aren't you coming?

"Oh! That meeting. Of course, I am coming. I'll see you there."

The snail went on its way while the cock continued to play. A few minutes later, the goat came along "*meying meying*" and met the cock playing. The goat had left early in order to eat some grass on its way. Since biblical times, the goat was used as a symbol of sacrifice and so it is that man continues to use the goat for offering. He has domesticated it and kills it whenever there is an important occasion. The goat did not know the subject of the meeting, but since it was the king of the jungle that had called the meeting, he decided to attend.

"Hi, cock."

"Hi, goat. Going to the meeting already?"

"Yes. Do you want to walk with me?"

"No, thank you. I will meet you there."

So onwards the goat went.

Next, came the giraffe. The giraffe is by far the world's tallest animal. Called the most graceful giant, it can grow to a height of over six meters and weighs about 1,600 kilograms, but it moves with such grace that were it not for the calmness of its nature, it could easily have been the king of the jungle. The giraffe could hardly be used for sacrifice because one powerful kick from the hind leg of a giraffe can kill a lion, let alone a man. However, man lays traps for the giraffe in order to use its fur and eat its meat.

The giraffe met the cock on his way and stopped to chat.

"Hi, cock," the giraffe said.

"Hi, giraffe. Are you on your way to the meeting?"

"Yes. Do you want to come with me?"

"No, thank you. I'll meet you there," the cock replied and continued to do what he was doing.

The cow came along and met the cock playing.

"Hi, cow. Don't tell me you are going to the meeting."

"Exactly," answered the cow. "Aren't you coming? You could keep me company, you know."

"I will meet you there," the cock answered.

"What is so interesting that is keeping you? If you linger too long you might be late," the cow said.

"Don't worry about me," the cock answered. "If I see that I am going to be late then I can fly. I will meet you there."

"Moo, moo," said the cow and continued on his way, and the cock continued to look for seeds to eat.

The tortoise is one of the smartest animals around. It walks on its short stunted legs and moves very slowly because its hard shell is quite heavy. The tortoise did not have to go to the meeting because at no time had a tortoise been used for sacrifice. However, as mischievous as the tortoise is, it is still an obedient animal. Since the king of the jungle had summoned a meeting, he would attend, even if it were just for the fun of it. The tortoise came along and said, "Hi, cock, are you not going to the meeting?"

"Oh, sure. But there is still plenty of time. I will meet you there."

"What if you don't make it?" the tortoise asked.

"Then whatever decision you take there will be okay with me."

"Stupid bird," the tortoise said under his breath, "at the rate at which man kills them, he should have been the first to be at the meeting grounds." And then the tortoise simply said, "Okay," and moved along at its slow pace.

"Coo, coo," the sparrow came flying and stopped to chat and share his meal with the cock.

"Why are you going so early?" asked the cock.

"Because I have many stops on the way," answered the sparrow.

"I'll meet you there," announced the cock.

Other animals met the cock on their way to the meeting and asked similar questions and got the same kind of response.

\*\*\*

To the animals, time is not measured in the same way that man measures time. The scheduled time for the meeting in animal language was just before sun set so that the meeting could end and give the animals ample time to go about their nightly duties. The lion looked at the sky and determined that it was time to start the meeting.

The lion is the undisputed king of the jungle, not because it is the biggest nor the most powerful or the most ferocious animal, but because lions are social animals. They are the only cats that live and hunt together in groups. The lioness does most of the hunting while the lion takes care of the pride. So, to fight a lion, one has to be willing to take on the whole pride. Thus, the animal kingdom bows to the lion by virtue of their spirit of togetherness.

The animals had come in their various forms and shapes and passed to the meeting place, leaving the cock behind. The cock stayed where it was, eating ants and playing. The other animals gathered in the clearing and the lion stood up and addressed them.

"Thank you all for coming. I am sure that some of you know the reason why I have called this meeting. For those of you who did not know and came all the same, I give you special thanks. The reason I called you here is for us to take a decision and inform man who among us he should use for sacrifices and offerings; otherwise, we will all become extinct sooner than later. As man's population increases, so will ours decrease if we do not work together to stop him from finishing us. What do you say?"

The hunt of the night before had shaken those animals that survived. There was no room for disagreement in the face of such danger, so there was consensus that it was a good idea. The question now was which animal they would choose, and how the choice would be made.

In the end, the lion decided to listen to everyone's opinion before they could make the choice. Was there an animal that would willingly agree to be the sacrificial lamb in order to save the others? If they could not come to an agreement, what would they do?

"Snail?"

"No way! We are not many and they eat us so much already. Let's choose someone else."

"Okay, goat?"

"No, not us. We do not give birth much and it will be easier to finish us."

"Cow?"

"No, not us. We are too big and expensive. Not everyone would be able to afford us. Besides, we provide meat and other things to man already."

They went through all the animals present and each animal had a reason why they should not be chosen. Then the tortoise said, "Why don't we propose the cock? He asked me to say that whatever we decided would be okay with him."

"In that case, we propose the cock," said all the animals.

***

The light of dawn was breaking. The weather was chilly and penetrating right through the animal fur that Fai wore. But he was feeling better because the hunt had not been as bad as he had feared. He felt the presence of the large animal besides him before he saw it. How could he have been so satisfied as to be careless? He stopped on his track to better assess the situation and looked into the eyes of a bear. As Fai watched the bear, he realised that he was shaking. Had the hunter become the hunted? The bear smelled Fai's fear and said, "Relax, I am not going to hurt you, at least, not today. I have a message for you to give man. We had a

51

meeting today and have decided that man should not kill animals randomly for sacrifices. We have unanimously chosen the cock. So, please, take the message to your people and leave the rest of us alone."

Fai heaved a sigh of relief as the bear turned and disappeared into the forest. But he stood rooted to the spot for a while to gather his equilibrium before continuing his journey home to deliver the message.

From that day, the cock has been used more than any other animal for sacrifices.

# Double Shame

S aint Theresa's Cathedral in Kumbo was the venue of the wedding which was the only exciting activity taking place on that second Saturday of August. The wedding bells, like the couple taking their vows, had come from America. The expectations from the wedding were high as it was the talk of the town for several weeks before the occasion itself.

The parents of the couple were well-known retired civil servants who were now enjoying their golden years between the village and the town. The idea to do the wedding in their village had been the decision of the girl's parents. The parents thought it was the natural crowning event of their thirty years of holy matrimony. Even more important to them, this wedding was going to give them the opportunity to celebrate and share their success with fellow villagers, although the young couple would have preferred to take their vows in the US where most of their friends would have attended the wedding. But they had bowed to their parents' wish and the wedding ended up with more of their parents' friends than theirs in attendance.

The central aisle of the cathedral was lined with a disposable red carpet and the walls and stands were decorated with flowers imported from America. If it rained, everything would be ruined. People would come into the cathedral with muddy feet and soil everything. So for that day, ushers and usherettes advised people to enter the church through the side doors.

The wedding was a mixture of indigenous and Western celebrations. Some of the songs were in the local language while others were in English. But the special offertory procession was traditional. During the offertory, individuals walked up to the basket nearest to their seats to put their offerings. A few members of the choir led the couple, family, and friends into the church. The two ushers leading the couple were dressed in traditional loincloth tied round their waists like sarongs with heavy beads adorning the clothes. Holding Saabs and cutlasses, they danced, moving to the rhythm of the song, dashing forward and backwards brandishing the cutlasses in the air and on cue, struck the cutlasses together to produce a loud clanking sound. The performance resembled a war dance. It was repeated over and over as the procession stepped towards the altar to the solemn beat of the music.

The bridal train was led by the junior groom and bride, followed by the bridesmaids and groomsmen, the couple, their parents and close friends who had gone out of the church to join the procession. The couple carried the wine and the chalice because that was the only day in their lives when they were given that privilege. The family carried goats, chickens, raw foodstuff and drinks. The wedding gifts were as extravagant as was expected. The priest came down to personally receive the offerings. Reluctant goats were dragged into the church, protesting with loud *meh -mehs* while the cocks crowed and flapped their wings as they were lifted up for the show. Most married couples in church took advantage of the ceremony to renew their vows or wondered if they could have done theirs in the same way.

Mr. Menjo, one of the invitees, watched the bride walk down the aisle, looking pretty and happy. He nudged his wife of thirty years and smiled at her then whispered into her ears, "If we had to do it again, I think we would do it like this. What do you think?"

"Okay," Mrs. Menjo answered, feeling very happy that her husband never imagined that he could have chosen anyone else, given another opportunity.

"Our Lem would make a prettier bride on her wedding day," Mr. Menjo said again.

"You can bet on that," his wife said, smiling at him and indulging her husband who loved their first daughter to distraction. Sometimes, the plans Mr. Menjo had for his beautiful daughter were, indeed, distracting. There were times when Mrs. Menjo thought that her husband had started planning their daughter's wedding before the poor child was two. It never occurred to him that anything could spoil all those plans.

On Sundays, while other parents relaxed, Mr. Menjo would gather little girls who had come to play with their daughter and say proudly to them, "You, you will be a flower girl for my Lem on her wedding day. You will be dressed in pink and all the other little bridesmaids will be dressed just like this," Mr. Menjo would use his hands to demonstrate the frilly gowns he dreamed the bridesmaids of his daughter would be wearing. Mr. Menjo dreamed of his daughter's wedding and planned everything down to the smallest detail.

Lemfon was not yet eighteen and had no suitors, but Mr. Menjo never considered the possibility that something could ruin his plans. He was the grandson of a catechist. His father had been a Catechist and Catholic schoolteacher. Their family was well-known and respected in the community. They had been brought up as fervent practising Catholics. He was now a retired lawyer. His six children had taken after him. He doted on all of them, but no one needed to be told that his first daughter was the centre of his heart.

\*\*\*

Three years later, Lemfon's parents were petrified with shame. Their darling daughter was reported to be pregnant. How could this happen? They had sent their daughter to a good mission secondary school. They thought they had brought her up in the best Christian tradition. So how could she have brought them so much shame? Not only had she got herself pregnant, they heard she was cohabiting with the 'author' of the pregnancy. Their daughter and this man had gone and signed at the civil status registry without bothering to consult them to perform any of the traditional rites.

Lemfon, their beautiful daughter, that calm and quiet child of theirs who was barely eighteen, already had a fiancé prior to being pregnant of another man! The boy was from their tribe and from a good family. How could she do this to them? Mr. Benedict Menjo blamed his wife as most men do when a child misbehaves. Mrs. Ancella Menjo kept her hurt bottled up inside her and wondered what she would do if she ever saw that child of hers whom her husband had banned from stepping foot in their compound.

The months went by and as the hurt and humiliation dimmed, Lemfon sent her parents a message that she had given birth to a baby girl and would be happy if her parents named the baby. After much thought Mr. Menjo named the baby, *Sevidzem*, which means, "Accept all". Then Mrs. Menjo decided to visit her granddaughter. She missed her daughter and wanted to see her. After much argument and pleading, Mr. Menjo gave permission for her to do so. With excitement and a high sense of anticipation, Mrs. Menjo took a week to prepare for the journey. She took some cobs of corn, husked them and ground the grains into flour. She shelled a bag of beans, harvested some avocados and oranges from their compound. Mr. Menjo plucked some kola nuts from the kola tree standing in the middle of their compound and tied them together. Then he went to his chicken pen, took time to look at the cocks and in one swift move, caught a huge cock and put it in a latticed basket woven out of dry bamboo sticks. He made a huge white mark running across the side of the basket for easy recognition. Once Mrs. Menjo felt she was ready for the trip, she caught a Bamenda-bound bus. Mr. Menjo had vehemently refused to allow any of his cars to take her on the journey.

The *Hiace* bus that was meant for twelve people now seated eighteen. Mrs. Menjo knew she was in for a rough trip. The bus rumbled on the dusty road and over bumps and turns. The police stopped them at Melim, a few kilometres from Kumbo. The gendarmes stopped them at Sob and Jakiri towns, which were barely three kilometres apart, then again at Ndop. At Bambui the gendarmes said someone's identity card had expired and the bus was kept there for over thirty minutes because the person refused to bribe the gendarmes. With all the stops and delays, the bus reached the beginning of the tarred portion of the road in Nkwen, a satellite town at the entrance of Bamenda, some four hours later. Mrs. Menjo was dusty and tired. One of the policemen on patrol lifted his hand and blew his whistle to stop the on-coming bus.

"Not another bloody police check," the passengers sighed. But of course it was another one. The policeman asked the bus to park by the side of the road, then checked the car papers first, and then everyone's identity card.

The driver needed to reach his destination, off-load his passengers and return to Kumbo. One of the police officers handed him the car papers and as he was about to enter the bus, a cock crowed and flapped its wings inside a basket. The policeman immediately stopped the driver and asked, "Who has the fowl?"

"*Na me, sar,*" Mrs. Menjo said, her tired voice full of impatience.

"*Wusai book for the fowl?*" the pot-bellied officer asked for the bird's health certificate in a hoarse voice.

"*I no bi know say fowl get for get book, sar.*"

"If the fowl has no documents then I'm sorry the fowl cannot be allowed into town." Saying this, the policeman untied the basket and put it on the edge of the gravel road. Mrs. Menjo watched as the policeman walked with a slight limp, carrying her basket to the side of the road. She could hardly believe that this was happening to her when she was so close to her destination. She was too tired to utter a word. It was not long before the other passengers started expressing their disgust at the policeman's attitude. The pleas of the other passengers fell on deaf ears. Mrs. Ancella Menjo now eager to reach her destination said if the cock was all that was keeping them there then they could as well abandon it and go.

Mrs. Menjo got to the bus terminal and the luggage was brought down from the carriage of the bus. She gathered her bags together and left them in the care of the truck boy who had helped her off-load them. Not knowing where she was going to or how far she was from her destination, she promised paying the wheel barrow pusher a thousand francs an hour if he could assist her find her way to her daughter's home. In her excitement to see her daughter, she had forgotten the inconvenience of the entire foodstuff she carried. She went into the bus agency and asked if she could be directed to the house of any Nso man. The agent she met was used to such inquiries from passengers, so he told her that he was from Nso and could direct her if he knew who she was looking for.

"*I di look for my pickin wey i name nah Lemfon.*"

"*Mammy, weti your pickin di do? You know wusai i di work?*"

"*No, i marry some man.*"

Mrs. Menjo could not believe what she was saying. Here she was, a former primary school teacher now standing in front of a lad, helpless. She could not imagine herself talking to this boy as if she was some uneducated village woman, and all on account of her stupid child.

How was Mrs. Menjo going to find her daughter? She did not know with whom her daughter lived or what the man's name was. All she knew was that she could locate her daughter through some Nso person, so she started asking for any Nso man and describing her daughter until someone finally led her to someone who knew her daughter and where she lived.

Mrs. Menjo was led on a footpath until they reached a house that looked like one of their boys' quarters. The house was built with mud bricks, roofed with corrugated iron sheets and faced another person's yard. Mrs. Menjo stopped the young man who was leading her and asked, "I am not sure you know the girl I am looking for. She cannot live in such a place. Where are you taking me to?"

"Madam," the young man answered, "*if we reach and no bi ya pickin no bi you fit lefam?*"

Mrs. Menjo followed the young man and came close to a young woman hanging diapers on a line. Mrs. Menjo did not know whether to cry or laugh. This could not be happening to her. Before she could decide what to do, her daughter turned her head, saw her mother and rushed towards her. Mother and daughter hugged each other in tears.

Lemfon heated water for her mother and took the water to a bathroom that was shared by other tenants. Her mother quietly took a bath, washed off the dust from her body, not remembering the last time she had bathed in such conditions. After the bath, she tenderly held her grandchild in her arms. The baby was so beautiful that Mrs. Menjo remembered the time she had held her own daughter in her arms in the St. Elizabeth's General Hospital at Shisong.

"How was your trip?" Lemton asked her mother.

"Tiring, Lem. I had the worst experience just as we entered town. The cock your father sent to you was taken by a policeman."

"You mean that Papa actually sent me a cock, Mammy? Has he forgiven me?"

"I should think so. A baby usually bridges any rift."

"So I can bring my husband home and introduce him to you people?"

"Of course, yes, if you want to be properly married. Why did you decide to rush into marriage, my daughter? Your father and I had so many plans for you."

"I hope marriage was included in the plans somewhere," Lemfon answered. "Wait until you meet my husband, Mama, you will like him."

"Of course, you know that your father always dreamed of walking you down the aisle to your husband."

"He can still do that," Lemfon answered.

"No," her mother replied. "We always assumed you would complete your education before getting married. Dan's parents knew that and accepted it," Mrs. Lemfon said, mentioning the former would-be son-in-law.

Mother and daughter looked at each other as they silently decided not to bring up the topic so soon after their reunion.

"Mama, I love my husband. I hope you will like him when you meet him. Please, Mum, give him a chance."

"I can't promise anything until I meet this young man. You know if your father was not too embarrassed he would have had the man locked up."

"Thank God he didn't," Lemfon answered, "because I would have chosen him over Dad. Mama, I love him. He is a nice man."

"You keep talking about love, what do you at your age know about it?" her mother queried.

"Enough to know I am happy with him," Lemfon replied.

"Living like this?" Mrs. Menjo asked her daughter.

"Mum, please," Lemfon said, "he will progress in his job. I hope we will be as happy as you and Papa are. Wish me that, Mum."

"Lem, every parent's wish is to see their children happy. I wish that and more for you."

***

The sun was setting and Mrs. Menjo was still contentedly holding her granddaughter and singing lullabies to her:
"*Oh oh la'a dze tong. Oh oh la'a dze tong. Ma'ati Mamie wii fo kwa, oh oh la la oh la oh.*"
"*Oh oh la'a dze tong. Oh oh la'a dze tong. Ma'ati Mamie wii fo kwa, oh oh la la oh la oh.*"
The baby was sound asleep but Mrs. Menjo was still holding her on her lap, not ready to put her in the cot.

A cock crowed and Mrs. Menjo looked up. A policeman, holding a basket that looked like her chicken basket, walked towards the house. Mrs. Menjo blinked, then blinked again. She recognised the basket and the policeman who had taken her fowl. She could see the white line on the side of the basket and the slight limp of the policeman. What was he up to, coming this way?

He walked right up to the house and then Lemfon came out to meet him with a kiss. Mrs. Menjo's head was throbbing with anger, shock and amazement. This could not be happening to her.

"Please, Lord, let this not be my son-in-law," she prayed quietly.

As if in a dream Mrs. Menjo heard him say, "Darling, I brought you a chicken."

"Oh! Thanks. That's wonderful because my mother is here."

He turned to be introduced to his mother-in-law and looked into the eyes of the woman whose chicken he had taken. The basket dropped from his hand as Mrs. Menjo stared at him. Mrs. Menjo recovered first then said quite calmly, "So, you are the young man who stole my daughter's heart?"

Ben stammered a reply but nothing came out. Without raising her hand Mrs. Menjo said, "Nice to meet you." That loosened his voice and he was able to say, "Nice to meet you too. Ma, welcome."

Mrs. Menjo had gone to Bamenda prepared to stay for a minimum of a month. So when she returned within a week, there was a stir. Women came to visit her when they heard she had returned. Some teased her: "Even at this age, you could not bear to be away from your husband for too long?" Mrs. Menjo could only reply, "And give some young woman the opportunity to lure him away from me? No way!" However, when the women asked how the baby was, Mrs. Menjo replied with a smile, "Fine, thank you," and went on to say in reminiscence, "She looks so much like her mother that I almost imagined I was that age holding my daughter again."

"And her mother?" the other women asked.

"Fine," Mrs. Menjo replied with a sad smile.

"And the baby's father?" the women further asked.

"They are all fine, only that my daughter is married to a thief."

# A Matter of Conscience

On the afternoon of that fateful day in May, it was hot and sticky. The air conditioner in the house in the highbrow neighbourhood of Bastos rumbled at full blast. The man was pumping away on the woman lying underneath him, up, down, up, down, unaware of anything or anyone else. He was about to enter heaven and could not be bothered about the world around him. He orgasmed, screamed at the pleasure, mumbled a few stupid words and slumped on the woman, a contented smile on his face. As he turned to position himself better to hold her, he saw his wife slowly closing their bedroom door.

"Oh! Oh! My God!" he exclaimed, not in the voice of someone who was relishing having been to heaven, but rather like someone shocked by a certain reversal of fortunes.

"What is it?" the woman asked him.

"My wife is back home," he answered.

"I thought you said she wouldn't be back for a few hours. What do we do now? How do I get out of here?" she asked, her lips quivering, her body trembling like a first-time thief caught in the act.

The best pleasures sometimes are stolen moments, places and times, locked away somewhere in the inner recesses of one's mind either too precious or too embarrassing to share even with the best of friends. However, the notion of self-preservation asserts itself at moments like this when one stops thinking of the other and starts thinking only of self.

The woman looked at the windows. She could not use any of them to escape because of the protectors. There wasn't even time for regret. The man and the woman now looked at each other as if they were strangers. They both knew how they got there, moving from gentle teasing, light flirtations, and then to opportunity and convenience.

The first time had been a pure accident, after which they felt shocked and ashamed. They had not known how to face their respective spouses. But they finally did, and found out that nothing had changed. The lure of adventure and the excitement of risk kept them coming back for more. They could still be together and no one would know what was going on. What had seemed so exciting in the confines of dark hotel rooms now looked sordid in the light of intrusion.

The man's wife waited numbly in the living room. Had she seen what she had seen, or were her eyes playing tricks on her? Was it the woman she thought she had seen? The one woman she could have sworn her husband was safe with? Was her fragile world caving in on her? For how long had it been going on? She waited patiently, too shocked to be angry. Then realising the predicament the people in the room found themselves in, she got up and shouted at no one in particular, "I am going to the market." There was no one else in the house. The children were still at school and the houseboy had gone to the market. Then she slammed the door and left.

After the woman had left, the man stayed in bed wondering for how long his wife had stood at the door and how much she had seen. Why had she returned earlier than she was supposed to? Had something happened? Could she have suspected anything? Had she simply set a trap to catch them? He was seized with such remorse that he racked his brains for any excuse to give her. But what reason can anyone give for such betrayal? Should he go somewhere and wait for her to cool down? That seemed the best thing to do, but he had waited a few minutes too long and it became too late for him to do anything. His wife was back and he could hear her moving in the kitchen. He looked at the time and realised that the children would be home any minute. Knowing his wife, he was sure that she would not make a scene in front of the children, but again, he could not be sure of anything because nothing like this had ever happened before.

He squared his shoulders, walked out of the room expecting a battle, but all his wife said was, "I turned on the water heater for you. Why don't you go take a bath before the children return?"

After bathing and dressing, he came out just as the children walked in. "Papa, good evening," greeted the first child. "Papa, good evening. Guess what I got in my Maths test," shouted the second. "Me, first. You always talk first," challenged the first and continued, "Papa, our team beat the visiting team and I scored two of the 3 goals."

"That's good," the man said without having heard what the children were saying. "You guys run into the room and change so you can eat and rest, before you study," he ordered.

"Okay, Papa," the children answered.

***

The table was set. The man looked across at his wife. She did not meet his eyes. He wanted to talk, wished the children could disappear and give him an hour with his wife. He waited for an opening for her to say something, anything. But she sat there, serene as usual, acting as if nothing had happened. She was a beautiful woman, always had been, and looked even more resplendent under the circumstances. They had a special thing going on here. Why did he have to spoil it by looking for what he had right there with him? The problem was, he had not even gone outside. How do you explain this madness to anyone? If this ever got out, what would it do to the family? Why couldn't she say something, anything?

65

"I am hungry, aren't we going to say Grace and eat? Mama? Papa?" queried one of the children.

"Go ahead. Lead us in prayers," the man answered.

"In the name of the Father, and of the Son, and of the Holy Spirit. Bless us O Lord, and bless these thy gifts, which we are about to receive from thy goodness through Christ our Lord. Amen."

No one heard Papa echo the "Amen", and when they looked, Papa's head was still bent in prayers.

"Papa! Papa!" the children shouted all at once. There was no answer. He was slumped over. The food forgotten, the man's wife and children screamed. The driver and houseboy came in and half-dragged, half-carried him into the car and took him to the Referral Hospital.

On arrival, he was rushed into the emergency ward where the doctor on call pronounced him dead. His wife saw and heard all of this as if from afar. As she collapsed, she could hear her son speaking into the phone, "Auntie, tell uncle that we are at the Referral Hospital. We have been told that Papa is dead. Mama has collapsed. Please, come quickly."

# Run, Quick! Quick!

The Toyota car built for five people including the driver now carried four passengers in the back seat and three passengers up front, which was not really an over-load because sometimes the car carried four behind and four in front with one sharing the driver's seat. It was twelve thirty p.m. and the driver of the vehicle had just been informed that the gendarmes had just changed guard. That meant that he would have to pay again and he did not feel like doing so. Business had not been the best that day and if he had to give two thousand francs again then he might just have spent that day working for the 'forces of lawlessness'.

The vehicle had left Jakiri with so much cargo packed in the boot that it looked like an over-fed hippopotamus. The destination was Kumbo, just some fifty-five kilometres from Jakiri. If the police as well as the gendarmes had in fact changed guard, then the driver would be looking at spending more than all the money he had collected from the passengers as a result of the overload. He rolled on and as he passed his fellow drivers, he put his hand outside to ask how close the gendarmes were. When he got close to Mbinsha, he slowed down and asked one of the passengers to get out of the car and catch up with them after the gendarme post. That way the gendarmes would never know of the passenger overload.

Meanwhile, Lukong, a young man, was sitting at the roadside not far from the gendarme post, selling cigarettes. The Toyota passed Lukong, slowed down and everyone shouted, "*Run quick, quick, come enter!*"

Lukong got up, left his cigarettes and ran to the car, opened the passenger door, squeezed himself inside, and slammed the door. Without looking, the driver drove off with tires squealing. The rest of the journey was uneventful, contrary to the driver's fears. The other forces had not changed guard, so he zoomed passed without any problem. When they got to the village of Melim, the driver turned to Lukong and asked, "*Wusai you di commot?*"

"*I no know,*" Lukong answered.

"*Weti you mean say you no know? No bi you put da ting dem for back talk say you di commot for Melim?*"

"No," Lukong answered again.

The driver stopped the car and everyone stared at Lukong and noticed for the first time that he was not the man who had boarded the car with them at Jakiri.

"*Wusai you commot?*" one passenger asked.

"*How you bi enter this motor?*" another one asked.

"*No bi na wuna bi say make me I run quick, quick, come enter?*"

"What!"

"*Wusai you bi dey?*"

"*I bi de sell ma cigar for corner road for Mbinsha.*"

"*Then dem say make you run quick, quick, come enter, you di come say wusai you di go?*"

"*I no know.*"

Feeling very disgusted, the driver pushed Lukong out of the car and drove off, leaving him there to make the long trek back to Jakiri.

# Palaver *Mimbo*

The place does not matter. It could be a dark hole smelling of cigarette smoke. The tables could all be half-broken, the chairs scraped and the floors stained and dirty. The glasses could all be chipped at the mouth. But to the regulars, it replaces something, somewhere, which nothing else can be compared to.

The time does not matter either. It could be as early as nine in the morning, at noon, in the evening or after midnight. Sometimes the place and the clients determine the time and the atmosphere. Thus, it can be anywhere under the shades of trees with a few benches placed round a dusty floor or on wooden chairs in a village, or at a posh club in New York.

The participants are generic. They are alike, yet different. Regardless of their height, weight, or the size of their pockets, they all come together for the love of *"mimbo."* It could be the best whisky or the crudest of local brews. It could be beer or the foul-smelling and cough-inducing fermented corn brew. It really does not matter. Once the members experience an overdose of the *mimbo*, whether in New York, Paris, London, Kumba or Tiko, they always leave behind memorable stories.

When I was young, there was this popular song, *"Tiko drink Kumba drunk,"* referring to all sorts of scenarios - from letting the wrong man pay for a crime he did not commit, to paying someone else's debts. After so many years, we were listening to the song play over the radio.

I have always liked spending Christmas in the village. There is a feeling of genuineness about Christmas in the village that I do not find in town. This year, it was the same.

We were there, the children, my cousins and I. We spent the days cooking and eating or visiting; but most often, receiving visitors. At night we always sat by the fireside and shared stories as we roasted maize which we savoured with groundnuts while drinking sweet palm wine.

Two days after Christmas, we were doing just that when someone I did not recognise staggered into the living room. The gatekeeper came in after him, telling him something in the dialect and begging him not to disturb *"mammy"*. But I am sure even as he said it he knew it was too late.

The man wore dirty and completely torn jeans. One could not tell his age simply by looking at him. I watched as he staggered towards me and stretched out his hand. I keep an open door policy in my home, so I stretched out my hand to greet the stranger. I could smell him as he came closer. The smell was a heavy mixture of alcohol and some other thing he had taken. He shook my hand heartily and burst into a narrative in the dialect, half of which I did not understand. I looked into his face, trying to place him. The fact that he walked straight to me told me he knew me. As he talked, I looked at him. Finally, something he said jolted my mind and I asked tentatively, "Tobin?"

"Yes," he answered.

"What happened to you?" This was a young man who, to the best of my knowledge, was at the university. My mind was floating, refusing to believe that this was the same handsome boy, so full of promise, whom I had known as a child. I stared at him, unable to say anything as he laughed and staggered out. I followed him to the door. The gatekeeper saw him out. When he returned, I asked him to confirm if the man who had just gone out was Tobin. My heart sank as he confirmed the identity of the young man. Aunti Waan asked if I knew him and I said I did. In fact, I had known him since he was two. So he would barely be twenty-five.

That is how we started sharing stories about drunks we knew or those we had heard about. The first to start was "Maitre", a university student who usually has this serious facial expression. He was tall and quite lanky. That evening, he was wearing a red T-shirt and blue jeans with holes ripped across the knees. He started by asking, "Do you know Mr. Joe who used to live at three corners? He came home one day so drunk that no matter how many times he tried to put his key into the lock, his hands shook so much that he could not open the door. He left the key in the lock, fell in front of his door, and went to sleep. At night, he really had to pee, so he got up and opened his door, went inside his house, peed right inside there, then locked his door and went back outside to sleep." We roared with laughter.

Now it was my turn to narrate my own story. "There was a married woman who drank a lot. One day, she had a little too much to drink and got properly drunk. As she stumbled home, she met a mad man who propositioned her and she accepted. There and then in the streets, they started making passionate love and before long, a crowd gathered to watch them. With all the talking, laughing and shouting, the *mimbo* cleared from her head and the woman realised what she was doing. She never touched a drop of alcohol again."

Then Maitre said, "It is normal to see a man drunk, but an alcoholic woman is a sad case."

"They are all human, aren't they?" I asked.

"Yes," one of my cousins replied, "But it is more shameful to see a woman drunk than to see a man drunk."

"What gives the prerogative to a man?" I asked.

"Something about the way society is designed, nothing more. Women are just supposed to be more responsible," Maitre answered.

The argument would have gone further and definitely would have spoiled our fun, so we returned to exchanging stories about drunkenness while gulping down our sweet

71

palm wine. Auntie Waan was ready to tell her own story. This was very rare because Auntie was usually so busy taking care of all household affairs and everyone else's needs, except hers. However, for once, she was sitting round the fire with us and actually had stories to tell.

"I heard of a married woman who used to drink all types of *mimbo*. One day, she mixed wine, beer and whisky. When she got up at night to go to the latrine, she passed out by the latrine and continued to sleep there until morning. When she got up and realised what had happened, she stopped drinking wine, but not the other types of alcohol, because she believed that it was the wine that caused her drunkenness! Can you imagine that?"

Maitre was nodding his head and seriously enjoying the palm wine. He came back with, "There was a man who drank a lot. One day, he drank so much that he fell into a stupor by the side of the road. Some passers-by found him, touched his pulse and felt nothing. Thinking that he was dead, they carried him to the mortuary and left him there. He woke up in the middle of the night on the cold slab of the mortuary. He stretched out his left hand and touched a corpse, stretched out his right hand and touched another corpse. My *contry people*, this is a true story! He started to scream at the top of his voice! On hearing someone shouting from inside the mortuary, the attendants ran away because they thought a dead man had come back to life. To this day, when the man sees anything that resembles *mimbo*, he runs for his dear life!"

Auntie Waan was on her third cup of palm wine when she broke out, "There was a man who wanted to marry a second wife. But he did not know how to break the news to his wife. So one day, he got himself quite drunk and in his sleep he mentioned that he wanted to marry a second wife. The woman pretended as if she had not heard anything. The next day when the man was sober, his wife slept and pretended to be dreaming. In her induced sleep she murmured, '*If second woman enter for dis house, I go commot.*' Realising that he had let the cat out of the bag, the man also decided to have his own dream. The next day he came home early, ate and promptly went to sleep. When his wife came into bed he also murmured, '*Man wey i no want banya, na yi go commot. Man wey i no want banya, na i go go.*' And having made his intentions known, he went ahead and married his second wife."

"So the dream did not work?" Maitre asked.

"Nope. Have you ever seen a woman who can stop a determined man from doing what he really wants to do?"

Maitre, who seemed to know many stories and was already on his third or fourth cup of palm wine, shared this one, "I know this man who used to drink too much. One day, after receiving his salary he took all his pay to the bar, drank away most of it until he got stone drunk. When the bar closed, he started staggering to his house and fell asleep by the side of a fish pond. On his way to work the next morning, his colleague found him asleep on the grass besides the pond. This colleague dragged his legs and put them inside the pond. The cold water in the pond woke him up. When he realised where he was, not remembering how he got there and fearing that some witches had put him there, he got up screaming and ran to his house where he got ready and left for work. Since then, he has never touched alcohol again."

Auntie Waan remembered this one: "One man left Bambili on his motorcycle to Bambui, a distance of two kilometres. He drank in Bambui until he got properly drunk. Then he climbed on to his bike and started riding back to Bambili. He went past Bambili and kept on going until he ran out of fuel. Then he realised he had gone fifteen kilometres past his destination with no money on him to refuel his tank. He had to beg for a ride back to Bambili. That ended his drinking spree."

"Oh," Lum exclaimed. "I know another motorcycle story. A man bought a new motorbike. He was returning home at night, drunk, when he saw a vehicle coming from the opposite direction. He started laughing, thinking that the two lights of the car where two bikes, so he decided to ride between them, and that is how he ran into a fatal accident. Although every single bone in his body was broken, there was still a frozen smile on his face."

She went ahead to tell the next story: "Do you know the story of this man whom the doctor advised to stop drinking? This man went to the hospital and after consultation the doctor told him that if he continued drinking he would not live for long. Then the man said, 'Doctor, not even a glass of wine? How can I live without taking even a little wine?' The doctor then conceded and said, 'Okay just a glass of wine once in a while.'

The man left the doctor's office and went to the first bar where he ordered a glass of wine saying, 'The doctor says I can only take a glass of wine. Can you please give me a glass of wine?'

The bartender served him a glass of wine which he drank. He moved on to the next bar. By nightfall, he had visited over ten bars in the community, ordering a glass of wine in each and repeating the doctor's orders. He returned home at midnight, lay on his bed without as much as changing his clothes. In the morning, when they came to wake him up, he was already dead."

Auntie Waan went on with yet another one, "There were two very good friends. One was rich and the other was poor. The rich man died and the poor one was very sad because he did not have money to contribute to his friend's funeral. After the corpse was taken from the mortuary and laid in state at home, the poor man went to a *mbu* house and drank all the dregs from every bottle he could find and got really drunk. During the wake-keeping in the evening, he dressed in a long white gown and came to pay his last respects to his friend's corpse. He addressed the corpse, 'Why did it have to be you to die? Why wasn't I the one to die? You know I do not have money. Who will take care of your wife and children? If I had died, you would have cared for my family. Now your death will bring suffering to all of us.'

As he spoke, the lights went off. He decided to join the crowd sitting outside, but as he went out, his robe caught a nail on the door. The poor man started screaming, 'Let go of me, Mr. Joe. I am not the one who asked you to die.' As he was shouting, the people sitting outside saw the silhouette of a man dressed in white standing at the door. They thought the dead man had come back to life, so they all took to their heels."

It was getting to nine and the village was quiet. Auntie Waan decided that it was time for the children to go to bed. But the youngest child who was only four said she wasn't going. They wanted to hear more stories. We all turned to look at them. What could they possibly have understood? Before any of us could ask the question, my eight-year-old son asked, "Mama, how do you tell if someone is drunk?" Maitre laughed very heartily, then turned as the gatekeeper entered the house. He pointed to him and said, "You see those two people over there? When a person is drunk, instead of two people, he sees four."

# Good Advice

Beri Lukong left the lawyer's cool office in Akwa Boulevard and walked into the Douala heat at two thirty p.m. She stood at the kerb, looked right, looked left, and started crossing the street when she narrowly missed being hit by a speeding car. The shout of the passers-by and the quick wit of the motorist saved her life. But it did not mean anything to Beri. She was dazed. She stopped one or two taxis but could not say where she wanted to go. The drivers looked at her in a funny manner and drove off. She started walking into the harsh glare of the light with no clear destination in mind.

Thoughts churned in her mind. *'Something can still be done. No, there is nothing which can be done!'* Beri walked and murmured to herself, her hands going so often to her head and unconsciously pulling her hair. Tears ran down her cheeks unchecked. She had walked for over two hours. Her feet were blistered and her clothes were drenched with sweat.

She found herself in Bonanjo at the "Place de L'Indépendence" and collapsed onto a public bench. She had to think. There was surely something she could do or someone else who could help her. The thought came in and out, floating away on the brink of her subconscious. A policeman passed by, stared at her and decided to walk on. But that jolted her mind. The police. They could help her. Her cousin's husband was the superintendent of police and chief of the central police station. She would go and see her cousin. Her cousin's husband should be able to help her.

She got up from the bench, a faint smile on her face. She stopped a passing cab and gave her destination which was only two blocks away. But her weary body and crowded mind were too weak to walk the short distance. Maybe all along, that had been her destination.

Kavi was preparing the evening meal when Beri walked in. Kavi was shocked at Beri's appearance. Her first thought upon seeing her cousin all dishevelled and with blistered feet, was that some relative was dead.

"Who has died?" Kavi asked.

"No one I know of," Beri answered.

"Then what is the problem? I almost had a heart attack when I saw you," Kavi said.

"It's a long story," Beri replied.

"Then I insist you shower, change your clothes and eat something before you tell me whatever it is," Kavi said authoritatively.

"But..." Beri started to say.

"No buts! Nothing can be that bad. You can wear one of my *kabas*," Kavi said.

"Thanks," Beri answered.

Revived by the shower and food, Beri launched into her narrative. Kavi listened to her very attentively. At the end of Beri's narrative, Kavi took a deep breath and said, "Well, instead of going to the police about this issue, here is the best advice I can give you. Do you know the goat market at Bepanda?"

"Yes," Beri answered.

"Go there. They usually have very strong ropes. Buy one, and then go hang yourself," Kavi said.

"What?" Beri asked.

"That is the only advice I can give you," Kavi said.

"What?" Beri asked again, not believing her ears.

"I cannot believe that a young, intelligent, and educated girl like you, could take her hard-earned money, buy a taxi, a house and much more in her boyfriend's name; you both have some stupid argument and now he has taken off with everything leaving you for dead. What sort of advice can I give you? I do not see anything else you can do. Go and hang yourself," Kavi said.

Beri Lukong got up and walked out without glancing backwards.

# Die na Kongosa

The stunned silence which followed Mrs. Kinyuy's declaration that her husband could never do such a thing should have served as some kind of forewarning to her. But it did not. She had stated emphatically amongst a group of women that for the fifteen years she had been married to her husband, she had never known him to have a mistress nor look at any other woman. She did not know that her world was going to come crashing around her with a mighty bang barely two weeks later!

It was four o'clock on that October day in Douala. The heat was quite stifling and the air came to a standstill as Mrs. Kinyuy stood over the wooden fireside to stir the corn flour that was cooking in the soot-coated pot. She opened the pot, added water for the third time and let it cook for a few minutes before churning it. She wiped the sweat from her face with the back of her hand, cursed the heat, and opened the pot to mix the flour for the last time. That was the way her husband liked his fufu corn, not too soft, not too hard either. She had to do it just right and keep it hot in the food flask otherwise he would come home and complain about the food.

Mrs. Kinyuy smiled as she realised that the food had reached the right consistency. As she shouted at the housegirl to bring the flask, a car hooted at her gate. The housegirl also heard the hoot but hesitated because she could not decide if she should open the gate first or take the food flask to her mistress. Her mistress would shout at her if she delayed because she should have brought the flask and kept it by the wooden kitchen before she started cooking. As the housegirl hesitated, Mrs. Kinyuy shouted at her to hurry up with the flask because she could already smell a slight burn of the *fufu*. If it got burnt, then it meant she had to do the cooking all over and it would not be pleasant at all in the heat. In the end, Mrs. Kinyuy got up to go and take the food flask herself while the girl opened the gate. She forgot all about the food on the fire and the flask when she heard the voices of the people who were asking for her. It was neither her children nor her husband. What had happened to them?

There were three people, two policemen and Robert, her husband's closest friend. As the smell of burning *fufu* filled the living room, Mrs. Kinyuy looked from the policemen to her husband's friend and waited for one or the other to say something. Finally, unable to stand the suspense any longer, she asked, "Robert, what is it? Has something happened to my husband or to the children?"

"I think you should sit down first," Robert replied, "We do have something of a delicate nature to tell you."

"Okay," she replied, "why don't we go into the other sitting room?"

***

After they sat down, the policemen looked at Robert and Robert looked at the policemen. The suspense was too much for Mrs. Kinyuy. She sat there, rubbing her palms together and silently praying.

Robert took a deep breath and said, "I don't know how to tell you this, but you have to be brave."

"My husband is not in any trouble with the police, is he?"

"No," Robert answered, "it is worse than that. Paul is dead."

"What? Has there been an accident?"

"Something like that, madam," one of the policemen interjected. "Your husband was found dead in a hotel room in town and we need you to come and identify him and decide what to do with the corpse."

"There has to be some kind of mistake here. My husband left home this morning for work. He could not be in a hotel!"

"I have seen him, Martha. It's Paul alright."

Shaking her head, Mrs. Kinyuy said, "No. What would he be doing in a hotel room during working hours?"

"Madam, is there a relative of your husband's whom you will like us to contact? Some decisions have to be taken fast."

Mrs. Kinyuy looked at Robert and the two policemen; finding no relief from them, she said, "Bob, let's call Paul's uncle and sister."

"I think his uncle would be fine."

"Okay," she replied.

***

Mr. Kinyuy's body was sprawled naked across the bed, his buttocks pointing up while his arms hung loosely besides him. Mrs. Kinyuy stifled a scream as the lifeless face of her husband was revealed to her. The air conditioner in the room was still humming away as the policemen hovered around with papers in their hands. Mrs. Kinyuy would have collapsed but for the timely support of Robert who held her and led her to the only chair in the room. A few minutes later, Paul's uncle arrived and the policemen gave him a brief description of what they thought had happened.

Mrs. Kinyuy caught bits of the conversation. Her husband had been making love to a woman when he suddenly slumped over her. The woman panicked, ran out, called the police and Robert, and then disappeared. Whether Mr. Kinyuy would have lived had he received immediate medical attention, was anyone's guess. The family had to decide whether to make it a public matter by opening up an inquiry or keep it quiet and bury him. It really did not matter because somehow the story would still leak, but Mrs. Kinyuy opted to preserve what little honour the family still had by dealing quietly with the matter. The police finished jotting down their notes and the body was moved to the mortuary of the Referral Hospital.

By the time they completed the formalities, news of the death of her husband had spread and there were already people waiting for her at home. When she saw people sitting in her house crying and shouting, she suddenly realised that she was not in some nightmare from which she would wake up. She burst into tears and wailed continuously. The children gathered round her with wet and dripping eyes, asking her what had happened and not understanding anything. How could their father with whom they had driven to school together that morning be dead before they returned from school?

"What happened?"

"Was he sick?"

"How did he die?"

It was good to keep things quiet but what was she supposed to tell friends and family? Mrs. Kinyuy was as mad as a bull. At forty, she was already a widow and her four boys had just become orphans. She was angry that her husband was dead. Everyone had to die sometime or another. But no one had the right to die such a shameful death. Why did he have to go and die while making love to another woman? He had left his wife not only confused but also angry because she was so ill prepared. And what about the shame that would follow them? As the news spread, friends and family came to condole with her and so there was no such thing as sleep.

The following day, Mrs. Kinyuy had to go to the bank to withdraw some money because she had nothing to start entertaining people with, let alone make any preparations for the burial and funeral. Her husband had been the one operating their joint salary account in the bank. When she got there, not only did the bank inform her that they did not know her, but worst of all, there was no money in their joint account. She returned home frustrated and in tears. She had to depend on the largesse of friends and relatives.

However, Mrs. Kinyuy had to prepare for the funeral. She had no money and did not know where to start. When people came to condole with her, she cried and cried and everyone thought she was mourning the passing away of her husband. But most of the tears were actually flowing from her embarrassment that she was unable to offer sympathisers anything to eat or drink. How or where was she going to start? Her husband was a director at the government-run telephone company. It was not expected that his corpse would be buried in a cheap coffin. Where was she going to get the money to buy a coffin, let alone entertain people? Her friends came to console her; and while she was wailing, one woman came to her and said, "*Listen, wipe dat ya eye dem. People dem need for chop and drink. How many crate mimbo you want say make dem buy?*"

Another one came and asked Mrs. Kinyuy, "*How many bunch planti you want say make I make arrangement for buyam?*"

Yet another woman told her, "*Dat cry wey you di cry so no mean anything eh? Tie your heart, bury your man fine, after people dem don go, then you fit cry. Come tell me weti you want say make dem cook.*"

Each well-meaning advice brought more pain. How could she explain to these friends that she had nothing and did not know where to turn to? As news of the death continued to spread, more people came with cooked food. Some people gave Mrs. Kinyuy money to entertain visitors. Her brother-in-law came in and began shouting, "*My brother eh, my brother eh, na weti kill yi eh? Weti I go do?*" Five minutes later, he called Mrs. Kinyuy into the room and asked, "*Wusai my brother i bank book dem dey?*"

85

*"I no know wusai dem dey."*

*"You don hide de book so that you go chop all dat money you one.
No bi so?"*

Mrs. Kinyuy looked at her brother-in-law as if she was
seeing him for the first time. This was her husband's younger
brother who had lived with them all his school life, had
completed university under her roof, and was now a teacher.
Did she hear him right? She wiped her eyes, counted from
one to ten silently and told him, "As a matter of fact, if you
know where there is any bank book, please, go and look for
it because as I stand here I do not have a franc to prepare
for your brother's funeral. You had better go out and start
looking for your own contribution for the arrangements."

"You expect me to believe that?" he replied.

"Frankly speaking, I do not care if you believe me or
not. It just so happens that it is the truth. I would further
suggest that you wait for the rest of the family members to
come for us to make the arrangements."

"That is going to be your attitude eh? *We go see!*" he
threatened and walked out of the room. Mrs. Kinyuy sat on
her bed, shaking. How could she have raised her brother-
in-law, treated him like her own brother, without realising
just what kind of a person he was? She suddenly felt cold.
She had once been told that no matter how well you treat
your in-laws, you will never know their true colours until
you become a widow. What was in store for her besides the
fact that she was now a widow without a dime to mourn
her husband? She looked at the bedroom and suddenly
noticed the old over-washed and used-out sheets on the
same bed they had slept in for all her married life. How
come she never noticed how shabby the room looked? She
got up, changed the old beddings for new ones, and then
tidied the room.

When the news of Mr. Kinyuy's death reached his
colleagues the following morning, management sent a

delegation to come and assist Mrs. Kinyuy with the funeral arrangements. The company was going to take care of most of the bills, including transportation of the corpse and family to the village. Mrs. Kinyuy almost smiled with relief before she caught herself in time. As a widow, she was not supposed to smile. Putting on the appropriate countenance, she thanked the company's administration.

The family and very close friends held a meeting and decided to have the burial the following weekend. The meeting was scheduled in the afternoon when most sympathisers would be at work. Mr. Kinyuy's uncle, sister, two brothers, a cousin, Robert, and Mrs. Kinyuy's two relatives were present. Although she was legally the principal concerned party, she would have to listen rather than talk.

"How soon can the burial be arranged?" Robert asked.

"It would depend on the finances available," the uncle said.

They turned to look at Mrs. Kinyuy who said, "I do not have any money, and this morning when I went to the bank, I was told there was nothing in our joint account."

Her brother-in-law turned, looked at the sister as if to say, "Did I not tell you?"

"Excuse me," the sister-in-law said, "My brother is not yet buried and his money is already finished. Tell us something else. By the way, I didn't hear my brother was sick. I have only heard he has died. Can you tell me what killed him?"

There was silence as everyone looked at each other with the air as thick as mountaintop fog on a rainy morning. Mr. Kinyuy's uncle hushed his niece and then decided that since it was a small group, the truth had to be explained to them. And then he declared, "Let's see how much we can put together between us before we decide when we can schedule the burial."

They settled down to continue the discussions but brother and sister both declared that they had no money. "Well, let's write down what needs to be done and assign duties to everyone. But since we do not have money today, which is already Wednesday, I do not see how we can have the burial this weekend. So I suggest we start looking at the following weekend." The suggestion was agreed upon, but Mrs. Kinyuy still worried about logistics.

It all meant that people would be coming to Mrs. Kinyuy's home daily for over a week. They would need to be fed and entertained and Mrs. Kinyuy did not know how she was going to do that. Individuals came and gave her money which she recorded in an exercise book. *Die na njangi*; what you give someone when they lose a loved one is the same they will give you when you lose someone in turn. Every gift had to be recorded in order not to be forgotten. From the money and food that people brought, the days became manageable, without many hassles concerning food or drinks.

Funerals usually attract people from all walks of life and backgrounds. Nowhere else is one likely to see people they have not seen for years than at a funeral. And more so, people attend funerals for all sorts of reasons. Some, for the friendship they feel towards the family; others, because one or another member of that family had come to theirs; some, because they have nothing better to do; and others because they will get a bite and a drink. As such, funeral services are usually rife with gossip, speculation, and skeletons being exposed to public ears. Mr. Kinyuy had given more than enough reason for gossip, and it was cutting through the air. Mrs. Kinyuy had no illusions that her family would be the topic of gossip for months to come.

The removal of the corpse from the mortuary was scheduled for Thursday at three p.m. followed by the overnight wake-keeping. The following day they would leave for the village where there would be another vigil before the final burial on Saturday. Those were the days to seriously prepare for, because many people were expected to attend.

The crowd at the mortuary was over five hundred. Mrs. Kinyuy paid her last respects to her husband's corpse before it was put on the mortuary slab for the final blessing and to let others pay their last respects too. Only then would it be taken to the family home. Mrs. Kinyuy and her children, all dressed in white, sat on the front row and the priest was about to start prayers when there was a commotion and everyone turned towards the noise.

Approaching the casket was a woman also dressed like the bereaved, supported by another woman, pushing forward two children dressed in white as well. The two children were carbon copies of Mr. Kinyuy. Mrs. Kinyuy was too shocked to show any embarrassment and she could not create any scene had she even the energy to do so. Someone led the other woman to a seat and the blessing continued. Mrs. Kinyuy watched as one of her husband's cousins moved to welcome the other woman and her children. She had heard stories of wives who, while mourning their husbands, would be confronted by another woman showing up with children who looked more like the deceased man than the wife's own children.

Mrs. Kinyuy half-listened to the priest as she watched the faces of her in-laws. She could easily identify those who knew the other woman from those who were surprised to see her.

The all-night vigil was scheduled to start at seven with a funeral mass after which there would be a second viewing of the body. Refreshments and entertainment would follow the church service.

Mrs. Kinyuy was hysterical. She did not know whether to cry, curse, or laugh. Who was this other woman who had shown up at the mortuary and had followed them into their home? What should she do? Did it matter what she did?

Suddenly, Mrs. Kinyuy did not know why she was crying, or for whom. And this because the man she had been monogamously married to for more than fifteen years was not the man she thought she knew. How many more children did the man have, and how many more mistresses had he kept? If he had had time for another family besides those he so professed to love, then had their relationship not been a lie through and through?

Before the all-night vigil, the gossip about the other woman had already spread and that lured even more people than were expected to attend the wake-keeping. People came in singles, pairs and groups. Some waited. Others danced while a few listened to the choirs singing. Many ate and drank. But most often everybody found old friends. No matter how well arranged the sitting was, before long, people moved the chairs from one area to another so as to sit with friends and talk. And so it was that one group of supposed mourners sat at a strategic corner and as people passed by, they ran commentaries on their dressing.

"Wow, wow! Look at how that one is dressed. Hmm. Where does she think she is going to?"

"Which one? I have not seen her."

"Don't you see that girl in that tight black dress?" the other asked, pointing.

"That one talking with the man by the door? Does she think she is going to a party?"

"*Wu know? Sometime i come for find yi own man for here.*" They laughed and then turned their attention to someone else.

"*You know dat man wey i enter with dat woman now? De tall one. No, dat one over dere. Na drunkard, i don marry three time and divorce three time, and i get pickem dem for all side. I wanda wu dat brave woman bi wey i di want go enter trouble now.*"

"*You no know dat girl? No bi dat woman wey i bi die last year for Bamenda yi pickin?*"

*"Which woman?"*

*"Dat one wey i bi di commot with dat married man wey i bi die for motor accident?"*

*"Oh dat one. I no bi know say i get picken wey i don big like this."*

*"Oh ma mamie eh? Na dat woman i pickin fit di go out with old man like dat?"*

*"If some man no de for tell yi, I beg make I go tell de pickin say dat man get seven plus one."*

*"Oh God! No bi dat pickin too don die na die so?"*

Another group was talking about the widow.

"I hear the man maltreated his wife. Why is she crying so much?"

"You mind her? She is only pretending."

"Maybe, maybe not. But it would surprise you that no matter how bad a person is, when he dies, the living spouse always misses him," another woman put in.

Yet, another group, sitting at the back of the canopies with a good view of the entrance was also making their own contributions.

"Hey. Can you imagine the cheek? That woman who just came in was going out with the late man."

"What?"

"Are you sure?"

"Of course."

"How can you be so certain?"

"Oh, it was a common secret."

"The cheek of it! How does she have the guts to come here?"

"Where the other woman had the guts to go to the mortuary, of course!"

"The man must have been a *woman wrapper*. Yet, when you looked at him, he looked like he could not kill an ant."

"How many wives and children does the man have?"

"Who knows now? More may be coming out of the woods when they hear that he is dead."

"It says in his biography that he left behind a wife and four children." The women laughed loud and other people turned to look at them.

At another corner, five people sat - two men and three women. Near them were two bottles of wine and three bottles of beer. They ate chicken, some fried fish and meat pie as they talked.

"I expected this death ceremony to have more food than this."

"*Massa*, did you go to Mr. Kum's burial? There was so much to eat and drink there that people carried bottles of wine away."

"Did you look at the casket and the man's clothes?"

"*Lefam so.* You know that burial I attended in Kumba last week? The coffin was bought in the States. Those children spent so much on their father. Hm."

"Death has become so expensive now. You should just stop criticising until it is your turn," someone quipped.

One of the women sighed and complained, "*Wu cook dis chicken? Spices no even enter for inside.*"

At another corner two people stood close to each other - a married man and a single girl. The man was saying, "*Ha ah, I say eh? Why you di so so avoid me? I don do you something?*"

"Nothing," she replied, "*I hear say your woman sabi follow people too much. I no want me trouble oh!*"

"Is that your only reason for giving me the run around all this time?" the man asked, laughing.

"Isn't that a good enough reason? If you don't care about your reputation, I do about mine," she replied just as the man's wife walked towards them. The girl quickly walked off.

At the back of the house, some young men were barbecuing meat while a group of women from Mrs. Kinyuy's *njangi* were busy cooking and frying various food items.

"*I say eh? Wu know de woman wey i bi de for dat hotel with Mr. Kinyuy?*" one of the women asked.

"*I hear say na some yi old reliable,*" another countered.

Yet another woman clapped her hands and referring to the widow said, "*Die don mekam now water go seek yi level.*"

As the night wore on, people came in and went out and were replaced by many more. People who found nothing interesting at the wake-keeping drifted to nearby bars and chatted about nothing and everything as they drank.

And that is how at funerals, everyone's business becomes public knowledge simply because death comes knocking and the dead person can no longer get up to defend himself.

*****

As the convoy carrying the corpse arrived the village, there were palm fronds lining the streets from the main road to the Kinyuy family house. Mrs. Kinyuy burst into tears as she remembered the good times she had spent with her husband there. Her husband was well liked in his village because he had always been so humble and pleasant to everyone. He nurtured friendship with former classmates who had not gone further than primary school and integrated very well with the elderly. As they drove slowly to the house, villagers followed on foot and wailed. Family members waited in the compound where they had been sleeping since they heard the news of Mr. Kinyuy's death.

Some family members could hardly wait for the casket to be removed from the hearse. They shouted and fell on the ground. It took a while for some semblance of calm to return before the corpse could be taken into the house and placed for public viewing, paying of last respects, and mourning. The people of the city had mourned enough. Now it was the turn of the villagers. As soon as the casket was

**93**

displayed, the people who had come from Douala were led somewhere else to eat and rest before returning to spend another wake-keeping night of *Kongosa*.

Mrs. Kinyuy was still crying, wondering where her husband's concubine who had appeared at the mortuary in Douala would sleep. She was about to decide whether she should be generous and share her home with the woman when she was introduced to another woman with three children whom she had never seen nor knew anything about. Mrs. Kinyuy stared at her sister-in-law who was doing the introductions, wiped her face and went into the master's bedroom. If she did not lie down, she was going to faint. Who was her husband? What had happened to the man she thought she was married to? How could all of these women have shared her husband's life without her knowing anything about it or suspecting anything? How stupid had she been? Two of her closest friends followed her into the bedroom to console and advise her, but she simply shook her head. She needed to be alone.

The burial rites were to be performed the following day. The ensuing reception needed to be well coordinated, otherwise some people would leave without having had a drink or anything to eat. Mrs. Kinyuy was going to use all the envelopes she had been offered to give her husband a befitting farewell. She did not want a shortage of food to be another *kongosa* item.

Had she not been the official widow, the comedy at the graveside would have sent her into feats of laughter. The irony of it all was that her husband's company representative wrote a eulogy fit only for a saint, and ended it by saying, "Mr. Kinyuy leaves behind a wife and four children." But when the family representative read their own eulogy, he ended it by saying, "Mr. Kinyuy leaves behind two wives and seven children."

Friends and well-wishers left immediately after the reception. The public show was over and the private one was about to begin. That could turn out to be even worse than every other thing that had gone on before.

Mrs. Kinyuy was left with her family members who were supposed to stay with her for at least a week until "the floor was cleaned" and her hair was shaven. But she knew she could rely more on her elder sister who was a no-nonsense-woman. Mrs. Kinyuy was required by tradition to sit on the floor in a dark room for seven days without bathing or talking to anyone except to other widows. Her sister who knew the tradition greased a few palms with some money and the women allowed Mrs. Kinyuy to sleep on a mattress.

Every morning at four, Mrs. Kinyuy's sister escorted her to the toilet. It was there that she bathed, changed her underwear, put on the same clothes and came back feeling refreshed, awake and able to start the five a.m. wailing. Mrs. Kinyuy was responsible for feeding the women who were with her in the *Ngai* and to send food to the men's house as well. Nothing she did was seen to be right. It did not matter how much food she sent or how much meat there was in the food, the people were never satisfied. She turned to her brother-in-law's wife and whispered, "*I say eh, why dey no di ask dat other woman too make dem come give chop?*"

Her mate laughed aloud before replying, "*Dey know na only you because dey bi pay money only for ya head.*"

The hair shaving ceremony took place on the seventh day after the burial. Prior to this, Mrs. Kinyuy's sisters-in-law were required to beat her. So the one who had presented the other woman in the village to Mrs. Kinyuy lifted a big cane and was going to lash her with it when another old woman intervened and was struck by the cane. She stumbled and fell. Mrs. Kinyuy's sister came forward, held the cane, and screamed, "What is all this nonsense? Do you want to kill my sister because your brother is dead?"

"It's tradition."

"What kind of tradition?"

"She has to tell us where our brother is. Who killed him?"

"As if you don't know? Why don't you look for the woman your brother was sleeping with? She will tell you how your brother died."

People began shouting and quarrelling. Mrs. Kinyuy cried and silently cursed God to have turned her into a widow. She could not say anything since she was not supposed to talk until after the shaving of her hair. Pandemonium would have broken out but for the head of the family who came out of his house and shouted at the women to shut up and do what it was they had to do. At that point one old widow took Mrs. Kinyuy to shave her hair with a new razor blade.

After that she was taken to the river and washed with cold water from head to toe by other widows. She was then rubbed with palm oil and covered with a new *wrapper* which she would take off later and wear the mourning clothes of her choice. She could then start the real mourning process.

Two weeks after the burial Mrs. Kinyuy returned to Douala to go back to work and to enable her children return to school. She was very happy to leave the village, but how was she going to face the other women in her *njangi* group? She could hear her voice saying loudly, "My husband cannot do such a thing." And she lamented, "*Die*, what have you done to me?"

*Die* has always been *kongosa* because it lays bare everything about the dead person and more. But if only Mrs. Kinyuy had known that her troubles were just about to begin!

# Man No Run!

It was about one thirty a.m. The night was wet and chilly. Ngwe changed her position on the bed and wrapped the covers tighter around her. A few minutes later, she was woken up by a sound which was very low, but somehow this sound penetrated her sleep-drugged senses. Could it be a rat scurrying around the house? Her bedroom lights came on and Ngwe woke up to see three guns pointing at her head.

The men holding the guns wore cheap black leather jackets over dirty faded blue jeans. Their faces were covered with black stockings on which holes were cut out to make room for their eyes and noses. They smelled of a potent and unpleasant odour of cigarettes and alcohol. Ngwe felt the urge to vomit, but was too scared. One of the masked men put his hand over her mouth and said, "Shh...You shout, we shoot. Give us money."

Ngwe's heart was beating so loud and fast that she thought the masked men could hear it. She turned round to make sure that her daughter who was sharing her bed was still asleep. Then she replied in a voice which surprised her by its calmness, "*Wish money? I no get five franc.*"

One of the thieves answered, "*You no get money, eh? You want bi difficult with we?*"

"*No, I no get. If wuna bi tell me say wuna di come, I for bring some money keep'am for house for wuna. Wuna fren dem don come here so many time wey I no di keep money again for house.*"

"*Give we money,*" another one said.

"*I no get money for house, but if wuna tell me wusai and wen I fit meet wuna, then I fit bring the money give wuna for der.*"

The thieves burst into laughter. And one of them said, *"You tink say we bi fools, eh? You want set trap for we, no bi so? Give we money or we shoot."*

There were five thieves in all. Three of them pointed their guns at Ngwe while one moved round the room deftly emptying drawers and turning over boxes as he searched the room. The fifth stayed outside the house, keeping watch. One of the thieves began helping the other thief pack things, while the other two kept the guns pointed at her. She watched as they removed dresses from their hangers, took the TV set, iron, radio and other electrical appliances. One found a new printer, which was still wrapped in its package and asked, *"Na weti dis?"*

Ngwe replied, *"Na printer. But na govment printer wey I just bring'am for house for use'am work."*

*"Enh! So you bi one of dose govment workers wey dey di take govment cargo bring'am for house? We go take'am so dat you go pay'am. No bi you say you no get money? You go pay'am so dat next time you go know say you no get for bring govment proparty for yar house."*

*"But I no get money,"* Ngwe said and shifted to take a look at her daughter. In doing so, the cover lifted and her arms were visible to the thieves. One looked at her and said, *"Mmm...how you get fine body so?"*

Ngwe's heart pounded even faster as she replied, *"As you see de body fine so, make i no fool you. i don spoil all. I get AIDS."*

*"Lie. How you fit look so fresh den talk say you get AIDS?"*

*"Wuna really bi na tif pipu from out of town. All man for dis town know say I get AIDS. All ma fren dem don run me since dem know my status. Look'am for dey, na ma bag dat wey I commot for Yaounde for take ma mekcine."* As she was talking, she turned and discovered that her blood pressure machine was not by her bedside, then she told the thieves, *"I beg wuna, make wuna take everyting but make wuna lef me ma blood pressure machine."*

One of the thieves then called out, "*Commando, you take dat machine wey madam di ask'am?*" while the other opened the suitcase she had indicated and saw that indeed she had just returned from a trip and the suitcase was still unpacked.

"*For do weti dey?*" the one spoken to replied, then turned to Ngwe and said, "*You one, you get AIDS and blood pressure?*"

"*Na so some people dem dey,*" she replied. The search yielded eighty thousand francs which they pocketed and said, "*You say you no get money, look all dis shoes for you one.*"

The other chipped in, "*Tirer au pied! Tirer au pied! i go tell we wusai money dey!*"

Ngwe was shivering as she begged, "*No bi na wuna don say de foot dem fine? If wuna shoot'am, how I go do wear shoe and how I go work money for buy some orda ting dem wey wuna go come take'am?*"

"*Wusai key for yar moto?*"

"*As wuna don scatter house so, how I go know wusai wey key dem dey?*" Ngwe answered.

"*De car get radio?*"

"*Wuna fren dem for Douala bi don take the radio,*" she answered.

"*Madam, you funny eh,*" one of them observed.

"*Make we no worry dis madam. i don corporate,*" one of the thieves advised.

"*Wuna di make noise so, dis pickin fit wake up,*" Ngwe said.

In answer, the thieves waved their guns and boasted, "*No body no fit enter for yer.*"

"*Wusai yar charge card dey?*" one of them asked.

"*Weti bi charge card? I no get'am.*"

"*How big woman like you no get charge card?*" another asked.

The thieves completed gathering the items that were of interest to them and as they turned to leave, an alarm went off in the children's room opposite Ngwe's, and one of them asked, "What is that?" and moved towards the room.

The occupant of the room was a teenager. Ngwe's heartbeats jumped in octaves as she imagined what the thieves could do to the sleeping girl. "Oh, my God," she prayed silently, "please, do not let them hurt the child."

The thieves entered the room and found the culprit of the noise, which turned out to be an alarm clock. They said, *"We don over stay for yer. Make we go. Day don begin break."*

And so saying, they locked Ngwe in her room with strict instructions not to make any noise. With a final farewell of *"sleep fine,"* the thieves packed their booty in the trunk of Ngwe's car and attempted to start it. But it would not start. They then made the unanimous decision to collect the items they could carry by hand and so they abandoned the heavier items in the car.

Ngwe sat on her bed, shaking. The shakes turned to shivers and then she shouted at the top of her voice. She screamed non-stop until her niece and houseboy came and tried to open her door. The child besides her woke up and asked, "Mummy, what is it? Has something happened?"

Ngwe's teeth were chattering as she picked up the child and hugged her as if she would never let her go. The child wiggled in her arms and said, "Mummy, you are squashing me."

"Oh, my baby!"

Ngwe released her, not knowing whether to continue crying or to be hysterical. She thanked God that she had not been raped, beaten or even killed. However, she felt violated. Her bedroom which she always arranged neatly was in shambles. The strangers' hands had entered every drawer of her house. She no longer felt safe or protected in her own house. What would have happened to her four-year-old baby if she had been killed? Her niece was banging on the door from the other end and asking, "Auntie, where have they kept the keys to your room?"

"I don't know!" Ngwe screamed back. "Look for them outside. We may have to call a carpenter to come and break the door."

"Mummy! Thieves came again to this house? Why didn't you wake me up? I would have driven them away," her daughter said.

"I'm happy you didn't see them, baby," Ngwe replied.

"Were they masked, Mummy?"

"Yes, baby. And they looked frightful."

"Mummy, did they hurt you?"

"No, baby."

"Then thank God, Mummy, and don't cry again."

Lum and Niba found the key lying next to the gate. They opened the bedroom door and Ngwe asked, "Lum, did they touch you?"

"No, Mummy. I pretended to be asleep when they entered my room."

Assured that everyone in the house was fine, Ngwe called the police when she became a little calm. The phone at the police station rang for a long time before a sleepy voice picked it up and growled, "*Ouiiiiiiiii?*"

"I have been robbed," Ngwe said.

"*Ils sont toujours là?*" the voice at the other end asked.

"No," Ngwe replied.

"*Vous pouvez les reconnaître?*"

"No. How am I supposed to recognise people who were masked?"

"*Vous avez des ennemis?*"

"No."

"*Donc, tu ne connais pas quelqu'un qui ne t'aime pas?*"

"What kind of nonsense is this? I call to tell you I have been robbed and you ask me stupid questions?"

"*Nous n'avons pas la voiture, ni le carburant. Si tu a une voiture, tu peux venir nous chercher.*"

Ngwe got upset, abused the policeman and banged the phone. She called family members and friends to tell them what had happened. Together with her houseboy and niece they made an inventory of what had been stolen. Many people came to see her, listened to the story and condoled with her. Some praised her for her bravery while others thanked God for protecting them. One of those who came was her friend, Kaavi. She lived in Victoria, ten kilometres from Muea where the robbery took place.

After Kaavi listened to the story, she said, "*Mammy, ashia ya*. You were very brave. I don't know how I would have reacted in your place."

Many people were kind and sympathetic in their concern and advice. However, no matter what anyone said, Ngwe no longer felt safe in her house. The slightest sound at night woke her up. She cleaned her room over and over, but could still smell the thieves. Kaavi invited her out for a weekend in Victoria, but Ngwe who was very relaxed during the day, could not find any peace at night. Sometimes she would hear voices she thought were the voices of the thieves, or see a man and imagine he was one of the thieves. She shivered without cause and was tired and sleepy most days.

**\*\*\***

About a month after the robbery at Ngwe's house, Kaavi was asleep when she heard a loud banging outside her house. She suspected thieves, so she got up and called her houseboy to come and help her drag a ladder to her room so that she could climb into the ceiling.

The ladder had barely disappeared when the robbers gained access into the house and walked around pushing things and choosing what they could take.

There were six masked men in all. The thieves saw the houseboy and yelled, "*Wusai madam dey?*"

The houseboy replied, "*I no know.*"

"*No play with we. We go shoot you if you no tell we.*"

Kaavi heard them asking for her so she decided to try and get out of the house. She started moving, trying to reach the end of the ceiling and the roof of the house. She crawled from one plywood to another and as she put her weight on the ceiling, it would make a loud noise, *wow wah…wow wah!*

The plywood was too light to withstand her weight, so it curved inwards, creating visible cracks on the ceiling. The thieves noticed these cracks and began laughing. One of the thieves pointed his gun at the ceiling, fired a shot and said, "*Madam, we know say you dey for up der. If you no come down, we go shoot you.*"

Kaavi heard them. She was scared. She did not want to think of what the thieves would do to her if they caught her. She kept moving and as she moved, the thieves followed the cracks. Finally, Kaavi got to the end of the ceiling and decided to rest for a few minutes. She pushed the thin plywood separating the ceiling from the roof and was able to see, with the help of the street lamp, the distance between the ceiling and the ground below. It was a distance of some ten feet.

Kaavi took a deep breath, counted to twenty and jumped into the air with her eyes closed. She succeeded in reaching ground level, and that is where she remained. Her back was broken and she was covered with severe bruises along her arms and legs. Two of the thieves were waiting for her.

"*Wake up.go back into de house. We no want hurt you,*" they said, "*give we money.*"

"*I no get money,*" she answered.

"*No play with we, eh,*" one said, "*If you no get money, tell we why you bi di run?*"

"*Na fear,*" she replied.

"*Fear say weti? We tell you say we come for kill you? All wey we want, na money.*"

*"I no get money. Na de ting make I bi di run."*

*"Weti you mean say you no get money? How big woman like you fit say you no get money? Why you di stay for big house like dis? Give we money make we go."*

*"Wuna fit look for all side for dis house, if wuna see'am make wuna take'am."*

*"Madam, i bi easy if you just give we de money."*

One of the thieves slapped her, dragged her back into the house and left her by a chair.

*"Tell we wusai de money dey."*

*"I really no get any money,"* Kaavi replied.

*"If we fine'am see'am, we go kill you,"* one said as the others went round looking for booty to carry. The thieves searched and searched and found twenty thousand francs wrapped in a book.

*"No bi you bi say you no get money? Na weti dis?"*

*"Sorry, I bi forget dat one because na meeting money."*

*"Wusai other meeting money dey? We bi tell you say we mind wusai de money di commot?"*

*"I sure say na all dat wey i dey for dis house,"* Kaavi answered. *"I beg, wuna no kill me."*

*"Madam, you mean say we come all dis far for noting?"*

*Twang!* A slap sounded on her face, followed by another one on her back and she cried out, *"Wuna no kill me, I beg."*

*"We actually need for kill you for we time wey you don waste'am,"* the leader said.

The thieves collected all that they could, turned around and told Kaavi, *"We just sorry for you. We for kill you, eh?"* It was about two in the morning when the thieves left. Kaavi was in pain. She could not sleep; she could not stand; neither could she drive. She needed a doctor. She was afraid the thieves could still be loitering around and might shoot her if she tried to get out. So she sat where they had left her and cried. The houseboy tried to knock on neighbours' doors to ask for help, but no one opened their doors for fear of the thieves.

Kaavi was admitted at the General Hospital the following day. She called Ngwe from there and said, "*Weti wey i bi happen for you don happen for me too.*"

"Where are you?" Ngwe asked. "You don't sound alright."

Kaavi told Ngwe where she was and Ngwe left to go and console her friend.

When Ngwe got to the hospital, she found Kaavi bandaged from head to toe. She was propped up in bed with her back supported by stirrups. After listening to Kaavi she asked, "Why did you have to do a stupid thing like that?"

"I don't know," Kaavi answered. "I panicked and did not know what I was doing."

"Did you call the police?"

"What would they have done? I was in too much pain to add insult to injury by calling the police. *Next time I hope say I no go run!*"

# Crossroads

The alarm went off at a quarter past 6 a.m. Awan Anje sent her hand and stopped it, then turned on her side and went back to sleep. Thirty minutes later, there was a timid knock at her door. Awan murmured something, turned on her left side and went back to sleep again. She knew she had to get up. She must at some point because there were people who were depending on her to get up and work.

"Oh God!" she murmured into her pillow, "I don't feel like seeing my face in the mirror yet another day."

Today should have been a happy day for Awan. She was now forty-five. She wondered what there was to celebrate in a birthday anyway. Was it the fact that one was growing older, old, or being alive? If one thought about it, one could celebrate the fact that others did not live to see that same birthday.

Be it as it may, Awan knew all the reasons for celebrating her birthday. However, this birthday was different. She had always looked forward to adding another candle on her birthday cake. She had looked forward with anticipation and excitement to her eighteenth birthday and had celebrated her twenty-fifth with pomp. At thirty she thought she had started to live a fulfilling life. Now forty-five just seemed like decades too many. She had been too busy learning and making a career so much so that she had not noticed the passage of time. Now she was alone and afraid. She thought she had noticed the lines on her cheeks and forehead the previous week. And there were a few more strands of grey in her hair than before. Her body temperature fluctuated and the sweating was more frequent these days.

**107**

Did that mean she was not going to have the babies she had always wanted?

Awan's mind moved down memory lane and started replaying the tape of her life. She remembered her maternal grandmother who had been the first girl to be educated in her village and never let them forget it. She had pounded the essence of a girl's education into her namesake that Awan sometimes felt that she was living her grandmother's life, not hers.

What had she ever dreamt of doing? She liked school all right, but somehow along the line, she had always thought there would be marriage in there somewhere. The first proposal she received was just after she wrote her GCE "O" Levels and marriage at that time was the furthest thing from her mind. She had laughed the whole idea out of hand. Such things were old fashioned, she thought. Years later, when she met the man, it turned out he was a handsome man who could have made her happy. However, by then he was properly married and was raising his own family.

The second proposal had come from an acquaintance of the family who had quietly told her he was in love with her and she had been the reason he visited them so often. That had been her first year in High School. She turned that down too because she was so used to the man that there was no possibility of any romantic feelings between them. The man was also now happily married and working as a director in one of the big American companies in the country. There had been many marriage proposals before she went to the US to study. As a *bush-faller*, the attention had been great. She had received many more proposals, all of which she had turned down too. She had expected love, candle lights, butterflies and the romantic scenery, but this never was.

Awan was not a vain person but she knew she was beautiful, not only because heads turned when she passed but because she resembled her mother who was exquisite.

She wondered where all the beauty, the elegance, poise and education had taken her. Well, to a Section Head at the World Bank. So what? She was tired of all the glamour without the fruits.

At nine a.m. when she could no longer put off getting out of bed, she slowly lifted herself from bed. She picked up a loincloth from the side of the bed, smelled the fresh roses outside her windows, then walked into the bathroom. She headed straight for the mirror and stared intently at her face. There were no new lines anywhere. She breathed a sigh of relief and went about what she had to do.

After Awan took her shower, she slowly oiled her body and then entered her bedroom. She took a good look at her body in the mirror. She was tall, slim and very beautiful. Her stomach was flat and there was no fat anywhere. She smiled a little and opened her drawer and pulled out lingerie, the exact colour of her dress, and put it on very slowly, relishing the feel of the material on her body. The negligee flattered her body even more and she shook her head saying to herself, *a body any man would die for, but what am I doing with it?* She looked at the flat stomach she was usually proud of and wished it were wrinkled. Of course, it was flat because no baby had ever sat inside. At that moment, she would have given anything to change places with her friends who were fat, married, had children and were happy.

The tape in her head would not leave her alone. She shook her head many times to clear it. "I really cannot afford this kind of self pity," she scolded herself. She had a big meeting that morning and if she did not hurry, she would be late for it. *Does recent technology not permit women to have babies at fifty? There is still time, all I need to do is find a father for the child, someone whose status is HIV negative.* With that thought to comfort her, Awan dressed and went to work.

***

It was barely five a.m. David had been up for over an hour. He had gotten up earlier than he should have because he could not sleep. He went to his gym room, rode the treadmill for an hour, showered, read the Bible and went back to bed. Sleep was nowhere to be found. Besides him, his wife slept on, oblivious of all the noise he had made. His wife was thirty years younger than him. She was a beautiful looking girl and he had thought he was lucky she had accepted to marry him. He lay there thinking about his life as his wife turned gently on her side, a smile on her sleeping face. David sucked in his breath and thought, *"But God, she is beautiful and she is all mine."* Or is she? For how long? a voice asked him in his head.

David was surprised that his wife, Jackie, could be sleeping so contentedly. Last night, as always, she had turned towards him, nuzzled into his hairy chest and there was no reaction. He had held her tight, wanting to melt into her, needing to, willed himself for something to happen but nothing did. His brain and his physical need refused to merge and after a couple of minutes of futile attempts his wife had given up and gone to sleep.

But David could not sleep. He had heard about it, read about it, but somehow never imagined that it could happen to him. He lay in bed for hours thinking about it. He was fifty-four years old. This was his second marriage. He had thought everything was fine between him and the young girl who later became his first wife. The girl was from Mebena. He had taken her to America and she had turned out to be more American than his native African-Americans whom he had not wanted to marry. Here he was again with a twenty something year old, the mother of his two children. He had two children with his first wife and had thought that was it. He had never planned on having more than two children and God had blessed his first marriage with a boy and a girl. *God, how did I get myself into this kind of mess,"* David thought to himself. *It is funny how man makes his decisions without God, then blames God when the decisions do not turn out right, isn't' it?* a voice mocked at him.

David had been sexually active from the age of seventeen. That is, until last night. What would happen to their marriage if he could not perform? These were questions he needed to think about, but he did not want to. They could wait until later.

***

On the other side of town, Sango Mboa was taking a cold shower at five thirty in the morning. He had had an exceptionally entertaining evening and an even more enjoyable night. After work, he went out with friends to drink and chat. The waitress, a petite girl in her early twenties, served them their drinks, her smile a permanent fixture on her face. Out of nowhere, they had drawn bets to see who could talk the girl into spending the night and he had won. From the bar which closed at eleven, they had gone to a nightclub and spent two hours there before he brought the girl home. Sango smiled as he remembered with pleasure the antics the little girl hid underneath her small figure. The girl had just left and Sango could not wait to go to the office and talk about his night's escapades.

He opened his fridge and removed some sliced pineapples and put them on the dining table to thaw before he ate them. He put the coffee maker on and went back to his bedroom to bathe and dress. This was routine. He had no wife, thank God, but he had a housemaid who came in at nine and cleaned and cooked for him. Some times he never even saw the woman. He left his house at seven thirty every morning, worked until seven or sometimes eight in

111

the evening before leaving for home or some bar. Sango smiled at himself. He was almost fifty-six and felt as good as he felt in his youth. Well, that was besides the gout and sometimes the arthritis. His life could not be more carefree than it was at the moment, and he liked it. He had tried marriage once and it had not worked out and he was now allergic to the institution. He never could understand why people made such a fuss about being married and having a family. He had two children with his wife whom he considered his one mistake and he did not know how many more children he had with girlfriends when he got carried away and forgot to wear his condoms or when the condoms did not provide the much needed protection.

Sango bent to pick up a comb that had fallen on the ground and felt the pain again. He groaned and lifted himself up very slowly. He had been having this pain on and off for a couple of weeks, but he had not found the time to see a doctor. *I could fall like this one day and hurt myself. What would happen to me? Whom would they call to come and help me?* The thoughts came from nowhere and Sango did not like them. It was okay to behave like a foolish old man who commits adultery, as the book of Sirach would say, but how was he going to end his days? More than once, the girls he had picked up from the bar had ended up stealing his money. He had had to call the police once and still recoils from the policeman's remark after he found the money on the girl. *Would I have to be making my own breakfast and ironing my shirts? But I'm happy this way,* he answered aloud. *Then what would happen if you sleep one day and do not get up again? The door would have to be forced open? By then what would happen? You could get married,* the thought intruded. *But I am too set in my ways to live for a long time with any one woman.* Sango Mboa shook himself from those gloomy thoughts and finished his dressing.

Sango Mboa was tall, good looking and suave. He thought with good reason that he was irresistible to women. He had known few women who could turn down his proposals. That is, except Awan with whom he worked and who remained indifferent to his advances. He had been charming, he had been rude, and he had even stooped to pleading, but nothing moved the "ice queen". Sango could not remember the number of times he had had to go to the toilet because of Awan. *What made her so different?* Sango mused.

***

Awan was fifteen minutes late for the meeting. That was a first for her. Just as Sango Mboa was calling Awan's assistant for the third time to ask where her boss was, Awan entered the conference room. Sango sucked in his breath. *My God, she is stunning,* he thought, but snapped aloud, "This meeting was supposed to have started a quarter of an hour ago. Can you take your place so we can go ahead?"

Already feeling an erection, David quickly came to her defence with, "The girl is entitled to a sleep-in on her birthday, isn't she?"

"Not when we have deadlines to meet," Sango said.

"Happy birthday, Awan. How does it feel like to be one year older?" David asked.

"Fantastic, I should think," Awan answered with a smile.

"That's my girl," David said.

"Can we get on with the work?" Sango snapped.

"Of course, your highness," Awan answered, knowing it annoyed Sango when he was addressed as such. That set the tone for work that day and Awan could have cried with frustration, but she was busy, and there was no time for self-indulgence.

113

Awan knew that the two men found her attractive. One was not available, and the other was footloose and fancy-free, in her mind, not someone to lose sleep over. The other would certainly have been her type if he were not married. Married men were definitely out as far as she was concerned. She had tried a married man once, a long time ago, and the end had not been very friendly. The relationship had literally exhausted her. It had been with a government minister whom she had met and they were immediately attracted to each other. The man had called her until she had, against common sense, accepted to date him. At the beginning, they had met frequently, then suddenly, he would call that he was coming at seven and she would leave work early, go home and cook, bathe and dress and would wait for him, but he never turned up. At eleven, he would call to apologise. There were either unexpected guests at his place or he did not know what to say to his wife in order to leave. After three of such futile dates, she had had enough of the relationship and politely told him she could not balance the emotional stress as well as all the stress she got from work. Without missing a beat, he had snapped, "Then stop the damn work."

Awan raised her shoulders and asked him very quietly, "Just who the hell do you think you are talking to? Your wife?"

"You can be, you know," he replied.

"I know no such thing. To the best of my knowledge, you are a very married man or have you forgotten?"

"No," he replied in the same tone, "I haven't. But you can stop work and we would spend more time together."

"Really?" Awan asked, "In between your home, meetings, work and everything else? Thanks for the offer."

The man had not believed her but after he called a couple of times and she did not return the calls, he got the message. *That could have been a good relationship,* Awan mused. *Why is life always so complicated,* Awan thought as she sighed unconsciously.

**114**

"Now, what could be the problem?" David asked.

"Dreaming of some boyfriend, I bet," Sango said.

"Sorry, sir," Awan replied, "Not everyone has your one track mind."

"We all know that one track begins and ends with you, don't we?" he taunted.

"That would be a first, wouldn't it?" Awan answered back.

"I wish you knew that you give me sleepless nights," Sango said.

"Me, or anything in a skirt?" Awan queried.

David coughed to interrupt the exchange. "I think we need a break. We have been working non-stop for three hours and I can do with a cup of coffee. Anyone cares for one?"

"What the hell!" Sango said. "I think we all need the break."

"Well, I don't," Awan retorted, irritated at the way the men were making the decision as if she did not count.

"In that case, you can continue to work alone," Sango said as he walked out of the room.

"Lord," Awan said, "sometimes I think I can throttle that man."

David chuckled and said, "I think you two can tango." Awan glared at him and decided to stay put.

They still had not completed the work by seven thirty p.m. They analysed the data, looked at the report and were still not convinced. At a quarter to eight, Sango Mboa glanced at his watch, stretched, and casually said, "I think we should take the birthday girl out to dinner, what do you think?" David answered in the same casual tone, "Good idea. I'll pack up and meet you guys in the parking lot."

"I may have other plans," Awan said.

"Sorry, too late in the day now. Please, indulge me for once. It's your birthday. Let's not argue. Okay?" Sango said as he held Awan and gently led her out of the building.

The restaurant was not far from the office. It was built with red bricks and thatched with grass to give it a real traditional look. The inside was made of wild wood and the chairs were a mixture of comfort and nature. Potted plants separated one table from the other. The aroma was always a blend of cooking and flowers. There was something different about the restaurant today. The lights were dim and Awan could hardly see inside. She was about to ask Sango if the place was open that day when the lights came on and she faced all her colleagues singing, "Happy birthday, dear Awan..."

Awan turned tear-filled eyes towards Sango and behind him to David who had just followed them in. "Happy Birthday, Awan," they both said and each gave her a hug before the rest of the staff followed suit.

Awan had not expected that they would remember her birthday. She looked round. Was it her assistant who had set this in motion? Who had? It really did not matter because everyone was there. It was a Friday and a good day to relax. She opened her mouth to ask a question or say something and everyone said, "After we must have eaten," and Sango led her directly to the buffet table.

The birthday cake was finally cut. Did she make a wish? She could not remember. Some people had left and the small group that was left at the restaurant was dancing to the music the live band was playing. At some point during the night, Awan found herself sitting alone with David who turned to her with a very intense look and poured out:

You are a very beautiful woman...
I have never been fortunate to have a good partner,
One I could talk to and relate to,
One who could talk with me.
I guess I never would.
I am not a bad man, just a few beers too many though.
I am a good man.
I can separate the good from the bad and be helpful.

I love this country.

I love all people.

I would help every one.

Then he paused, bent his head, and left the rest unsaid. It was up to Awan to interpret. She looked at him, at a loss for words to say anything. Then thought:

This African-American who loved her country and her continent even more than she did.

He had one bad marriage behind him, while the scars were still raw and bleeding.

He got himself involved with a girl thirty-something years his junior, and now he is trapped in another marriage with two children.

She is a very beautiful woman.

He is lucky to have her.

But Awan could understand him and her thoughts continued:

What does an educated man discuss with a chick out of the nightclub?

Little education and nothing else?

But he is in for the long haul.

What else can he do?

He stands at the crossroads of his life,

Stunned about the things he has done.

Those things he would have liked to have done.

Those he might have changed,

And wonders where all the time has gone.

Sango Mboa chose that moment to return and ask Awan for a dance. The music changed from the salsa that the band had been playing to Michael Bolton's version of *Lean on me*, and as the band sang, Sango held Awan close and sang along:

Sometimes in our lives,

We all have pain,

We all have sorrow,

But if we are wise,

We know that there's
Always tomorrow.
Lean on me,
When you are not strong
I'll be your friend
I'll help you carry on,
For, it won't be long
Till I'm gonna need
Somebody to lean on.

Please swallow your pride,
Give me your hand....

Just call on me brother
When you need a hand,
We all need somebody
To lean on.
I just might have a problem,
That you'd understand
We all need somebody
To lean on...

Lean on me,
I want to be your friend,
I will be there for you, lean on me
I'm gonna be there for you, lean on me
When you need a hand,
I'll be strong, lean on me
Somebody to lean on.

I'll share your love,
If you'd just hold me
Hold me; Hold me,
Hold me; Hold me,
If you need a friend.

Hold me, hold me...
Lean on me,
When you are not strong
I'll be your friend
I'll help you carry on,
For, it won't be long
Till I'm gonna need
Somebody to lean on...

Awan leaned on Sango, her head placed on his shoulders. She could smell his masculine scent as she listened to the band and Sango sing the wordings of the song and wondered if she could dare ever *lean on him*.